# Hans Christian Andersen
# Fairytales

## Illustrated by Svend Otto S.

*Translated by Patricia Crampton*

**CARLSEN**

BØRNENES H.C. ANDERSEN
Copyright © 1972 by Forlaget Carlsen A/S, Copenhagen
Illustrations copyright © 1972 by Svend Otto S.
Translation copyright © 1985 by Patricia Crampton
Printed 1999 in Denmark
1. udgave, 10. oplag, 08.99.19/001004889
ISBN 87-562-3018-4

# Contents

# The Snow Queen

## *Which tells of a looking-glass and its splinters*

If you're ready, we'll begin. When we come to the end of this story we shall know more than we know now.

It all began with the work of a wicked troll. He was one of the worst of all; he was the Devil himself. One day he was in a very good mood, because he had made a mirror which had the power, when anything good and beautiful was reflected in it, to make it shrink to almost nothing, while anything that was worthless and ill-looking stood out and became worse still. It made the loveliest landscapes look like boiled spinach and the best people turn ugly or stand on their heads, with no middles; their faces were so distorted that they were unrecognizable and the smallest freckle was sure to spread over their noses and mouths. The Devil thought that was extremely funny. The best and purest thought reflected in that mirror became a grin, and how the Devil laughed at his cunning invention! All the pupils at troll-school, for he ran a troll-school, told each other that a miracle had happened; for the first time, they said, you could see what the world and the people in it really looked like. They ran all over the place with the mirror, until at last there was not a country or a person who had not been distorted in it. Then they decided to fly up to heaven itself, to make fun of the angels and the Lord. The higher they flew with the mirror, the more it grinned, until they could scarcely hold it; higher and higher they flew, closer to God and the angels; then the mirror shuddered with such terrible laughter that it fell from their hands and plunged to the earth, where it broke into pieces, hundreds of millions, billions and even more! Now it did even worse damage than before, because some of the pieces were no bigger than a grain of sand and they flew all over the world and wherever they blew into people's eyes, they stuck, so that people saw everything wrongly, or could see only the bad; for each little speck of mirror had the same power as the whole mirror. A splinter of glass even flew into some people's hearts and that was the worst fate of all, for their hearts turned into lumps of ice. Some of the glass fragments were big enough to use as window-panes, but it was not good to look at your friends through those panes; others were made into spectacles and things went awry when people put them on in order to see clearly and be just. The Evil One laughed till his stomach was bursting, which tickled him delightfully. But outside, little splinters of glass were still flying about in the air. We shall hear more about those!

THE SECOND PART

## *About a little boy and a little girl*

In the big town, where there are so many houses and people that there is not enough room for everyone to have a little garden, and where most people have to be content with flowers in pots, lived two poor children who had a garden which was a little larger than a flower-pot. They were not brother and sister, but they were as fond of each other as if they had been. Their parents lived next door to each other in two attic rooms, just where the roof of one house touched its neighbour's and the gutter ran along the eaves. A little window stuck out from each house; you had only to step over the gutter to get from one window to the next.

Their parents each had a big wooden box outside, in which they grew herbs which they used, and a little rose-tree; there was one in each window-box and they grew and flourished. The parents had the idea of setting the window-boxes straight across the gutter, so that they reached from one window almost to the next and looked for all the world like two flower-beds. The pea-tendrils hung down from the window-boxes and the rose-trees put out long branches that twined their way round the windows and leaned in towards each other like a triumphal arch of leaves and flowers. Because the window-boxes were very high and the children knew that they must not climb up them, they were allowed to come out in summer and sit on their little stools under the rose-trees, where they could have splendid games.

In winter there were no such pleasures. The windows were frozen solid, but the children would heat copper coins on the stove and hold them against the frozen pane to make a lovely peephole, round as round; behind each a gentle eye looked out, one from each window: they belonged to the little boy and the little girl. His name was Kay and hers was Gerda. In summer they could be together with one leap, but in winter they had first to go down all the stairs in one house and up all the stairs in the next; the snow swirled outside.

"It's the white bees swarming," said the old grandmother.

"Do they have a queen too?" asked the little boy, because he knew that real bees have one.

"They certainly have," said Grandmother. "She is in there where the swarm is thickest, the biggest of them all, and she never stays still on earth, she always flies back into the black clouds. Many a winter's night she flies through the city streets, looking in at the windows, and they freeze in wonderful shapes, like flowers."

"Yes, I've seen that!" said the two children, and so they knew that it was true.

"Can the Snow Queen get in here?" asked the little girl.

"Let her come!" said the boy. "I'll put her on the hot stove and she'll melt."

But Grandmother stroked his hair and told them different stories.

That night, when Kay was at home and half-undressed, he climbed on to the chair by the window and looked out through the little hole; a few snowflakes were falling outside, and one of them, the biggest of all, came to rest on the edge of one of the window-boxes; the snowflake grew and grew until at last it was a real, live woman, dressed in the finest white gauze seemingly woven from a million star-shaped flakes. She was both beautiful and elegant, but icy, made of dazzling, brilliant ice. And yet she was alive; her eyes stared like two bright stars, but there was no peace or quiet in them. She nodded towards the window and beckoned. The little boy was frightened and jumped off the chair, and, for a moment, a great bird seemed to be flying past the window.

The next day there was a white frost – and then a thaw – and then came spring. The sun shone, the leaves peeped out, the swallows built their nests, the windows opened and the two children were able to sit in their little garden again, high up on the eaves, at the very top of the many-storeyed house.

The roses bloomed that year as they had never bloomed before; the little girl had learned a hymn which sang of roses and those roses made her think of her own, so she sang it for the little boy and he sang with her:

"In the valley roses grow,
There the Christ-child we shall know!"

And the children held hands, kissed the roses, looked at God's bright sunshine and spoke to it, as if the Christ-child were there. What lovely summer days they were, how lovely it was to be out by the fresh rose-trees which seemed never to stop flowering!

One day Kay and Gerda were looking at the animals and birds in their picture-books when suddenly – the clock on the great church tower was just striking five – Kay cried: "Ah! Something pierced my heart! And now there is something in my eye!"

The little girl took his face in her hands; he blinked, but no, there was nothing to be seen.

"I think it's gone!" he said, but it had not gone. It was one of those grains of glass which had sprung from the mirror, the magic mirror, remember, the dreadful glass that turned anything great and good that was reflected in it into something small and ugly, while the evil and the bad became more distinct and the least fault could be seen at once. Poor Kay – a splinter had also entered his heart, which would soon become a lump of ice. It no longer hurt him but it was there.

"Why are you crying?" he asked. "It makes you look ugly! There's nothing wrong with me! Ugh!" he cried suddenly, "this rose has been gnawed by a worm, and look, that one is all crooked – in fact they are really horrid roses, just like the window-boxes they're growing in!" And he kicked the box hard and pulled off the two roses.

"Kay, what are you doing?" cried the little girl, and, when he saw her fright, he pulled off another rose and ran inside through his own window, away from little Gerda.

When she brought the picture-book out later on he said it was for babies, and when Grandmother told stories he was always saying *but* – in fact, whenever he had the chance, he made fun of her, putting on glasses and imitating her; he did it so well that he made people laugh. Soon he could walk and talk just like *all* the people in the street. Everything that was different or not too good about them, Kay could imitate and people said: "That boy's got brains, that's for sure!" But it was the glass that had fallen into his eye, the glass that was stuck in his heart that made him tease even little Gerda, who loved him with all her heart.

His games were quite different from before, they were so clever: one winter's day, when the snowflakes were falling, he brought a big magnifying glass, held out his coat-tails and let the snowflakes fall on them.

"Now look through the glass, Gerda!" he said, and every snowflake grew much larger and looked like a wonderful flower or a ten-pointed star; they were a beautiful sight.

"Look, aren't they curious?" said Kay. "Much more interesting than real flowers! And there is not a single flaw in them, they're quite perfect, until they melt."

A day or so later Kay arrived, wearing big gloves and with his sledge on his back. "I'm taking my sledge to the big square," he shouted in Gerda's ear. "The others are playing there!" And he was off.

Down on the square the boldest boys would tie their sledges to the farmers' carts and slide along behind them for a while, having a fine time. In the midst of their play a big sledge drove past, all painted white, its driver wrapped in a fleecy white fur and wearing a white fur cap. As the sledge drove round the square a second time, Kay quickly tied his own little sledge to it and slid along behind. Faster and faster they went, right into the next street, while the driver turned and gave Kay a friendly nod, as if they knew each other. Every time Kay tried to untie his little sledge the driver nodded again, so Kay stayed where he was until they were driving straight out through the city gate. Then it began to snow so hard that the little boy could not see his hand before his face as they rushed along; he quickly released the rope to free himself from the big sledge, but it was no use; his own little one hung on and they were travelling like the wind. He shouted at the top of his voice, but no one heard him and the snow fell and the sledge flew along, sometimes leaping as though they were crossing ditches and fences. In his terror he tried to repeat the Lord's Prayer, but could only remember his multiplication tables.

The snowflakes grew larger and larger, until they looked like big, white hens; suddenly they lurched sideways, the big sledge stopped and the driver rose, furs and hat covered with snow; it was a lady, very tall and straight and shining white: the Snow Queen.

"We have come a long way," she said, "are you cold? Come inside my bearskin coat!" Taking him into the sledge beside her, she wrapped her furs around him. He seemed to be sinking into a snowdrift.

"Are you still cold?" she asked, kissing him on the forehead. Ah! Her kiss was colder than ice, it pierced him to the very heart, which was already half made of ice; he felt as if he were going to die – but only for a moment, then he felt better; he no longer noticed the cold.

"My sledge! Don't forget my sledge!" was his first thought, but it was tied on to one of the white hens, which flew behind them with the sledge on its back. When the Snow Queen

kissed Kay again he forgot little Gerda and Grandmother and everyone at home.

"No more kisses for you now," she said, "or I would kiss you to death!"

Kay looked at her; she was very beautiful. It was impossible to imagine a wiser, lovelier face, and she no longer seemed to be made of ice as she had when she beckoned from outside the window. In his eyes she was perfect, he was not at all frightened. He told her that he could do mental arithmetic and fractions and knew the area of the country and the number of its inhabitants and she smiled and smiled. Then he thought that what he knew was not enough. He gazed up into the vastness of space and she flew with him, high up into the black clouds, and the storm winds rushed and roared as if they were singing old songs. They flew over woods and lakes, over land and sea; below them the cold wind whistled, the wolves howled, the snow glittered. Black crows flew past, screaming, but above it all shone the full, bright moon and Kay gazed at it through the long winter night. At daybreak he fell asleep at the Snow Queen's feet.

THE THIRD PART

# The flower garden of the old woman who knew magic

But how was little Gerda getting on without Kay? Where could he be? Nobody knew, no one had any answers to give. The boys could only say that they had seen him tie his little sledge to a fine big one, which had driven off along the streets and through the city gate. No one knew where he was, many tears were shed, and little Gerda grieved long and deeply. Then they said he was dead, drowned in the river that ran past the town; and oh, the winter days were long and dark.

Then came the spring and a warmer sun.

"Kay is dead and gone," said little Gerda.

"I don't believe it!" said the sunshine.

"He is dead and gone!" she told the swallows.

"I don't believe it!" they answered, and, at last, little Gerda did not believe it either.

"I shall put on my new red shoes," she said one morning, "the ones that Kay has never seen, and I shall go down to the river and ask it where he is!"

Very early in the morning she kissed her old grandmother, who was still asleep, put on the red shoes and walked all alone through the city gate to the river.

"Is it true that you have taken my little playmate? You shall have my red shoes if you will give him back to me!"

It seemed to her that the waves nodded strangely, so she took off her red shoes, her dearest possession, and threw them out into the water; but they fell close inshore and the little waves carried them back to her on land, as if the river did not want to take her dearest possession, because it did not have little Kay. She thought perhaps she had not thrown the

shoes far enough out, so she climbed into a boat lying among the reeds, and, standing at the very end of it, she threw the shoes again; but the boat was not tied up and her movements sent it out into the stream; she tried to get off but before she could reach land the boat was over a yard out, drifting faster now.

Little Gerda was so frightened that she began to cry, but only the swallows heard her, and they could not carry her inshore. Instead, they flew alongside the boat singing as if to comfort her: "Here we are! Here we are!" The boat drifted with the current. Little Gerda sat quite still in her stockinged feet, the little red shoes floating behind her, unable to catch up with the boat, which was gathering speed. Both banks of the river were beautiful, with their flowers, old trees and meadows full of sheep and cows, but there was not a single person to be seen.

"Perhaps the river will carry me to Kay," Gerda thought, and, feeling more cheerful, she sat up and spent hours watching the beautiful green banks, until she came to a big cherry orchard where there was a little house with strange red and blue windows, a thatched roof and two wooden soldiers outside to guard it from those who came sailing by.

Gerda called to them, thinking they were alive, but of course they did not answer; soon she was quite close to them, as the river carried the boat towards the shore.

Gerda shouted still louder and, at last, an old, old woman came out of the house, leaning on a crooked stick; she was wearing a big sun-hat, painted with the prettiest flowers.

"You poor child!" said the old woman, "what are you doing on the big, strong river, travelling out into the wide world?" And walking straight into the water the old woman caught the boat with her crook, tugged it ashore and lifted little Gerda out. Gerda was glad to be on dry land again, but she was still a little afraid of the strange old woman.

"Now come and tell me who you are and how you got here!" she said.

Gerda told her everything and the old woman shook her head and said: "Hm, hm!" And when Gerda asked if she had seen Kay the woman said that he had not passed that way, but he would come, Gerda must not be sad but come and enjoy her cherries and look at her flowers, which were prettier than a picture-book, each one with a story to tell. Taking Gerda by the hand, she led her into the little house and closed the door behind them.

The windows were set high and made of red, blue and yellow glass; the daylight shone very strangely through all the colours. On the table were the most delicious cherries and Gerda was allowed to eat as many as she liked.

As she ate, the old woman combed her hair with a golden comb until it curled and shone delightfully round her sweet, rosy little face.

"How I have longed for a pretty little girl like you!" said the old woman. "You'll soon see what a good time we'll have together!" And, as she combed Gerda's hair, the little girl began to forget about her playmate Kay, for the old woman knew magic, but she was not a bad witch, she only worked a little magic for her own pleasure, and what she wanted now was to keep little Gerda with her. So she went into the garden and stretched out her crooked stick towards the rose trees and however beautifully they were flowering, they sank down into the black earth and vanished without trace. The old woman was afraid that when Gerda saw the roses she would think of her own roses, remember Kay and run away.

She took Gerda out into the garden.

Oh, the fragrance and the flowers, every flower you could imagine, a flower for every season was blooming here; no picture-book could have been brighter or more beautiful. Gerda jumped for joy and played till the sun went down behind the tall cherry trees. Then she was given a lovely bed with a red silk quilt filled with violets and there she slept and dreamed as sweetly as a queen on her wedding day.

The next day she played with the flowers

again in the warm sunshine and many days passed by in the same way. Gerda knew every flower, but how ever many there were, it seemed to her that one was missing – which one, she did not know. One day she was looking at the old woman's sunhat with the flowers painted on it and the most beautiful of them all was a rose. The old woman had forgotten to take it off the hat when she made the other roses disappear – that's what happens when you are absent-minded!

"What!" said Gerda, "are there really no roses here?" She ran among the beds, searching and searching, but, finding no roses, she sat down and cried. Her tears fell on the spot where one of the rose trees was buried and when her hot tears soaked the earth the tree shot up at once, covered with flowers, just as it had been when it sank into the ground. Gerda embraced

it, kissing the roses and remembering the beautiful roses at home and with them, little Kay.

"Oh, the time I have wasted!" said the little girl. "I was going to find Kay! Don't you know where he is?" she asked the roses. "Do you believe he is dead and gone?"

"He is not dead," said the roses, "we have been in the earth where all the dead are, but Kay was not there!"

"Oh, thank you," said little Gerda, and going to the other flowers she looked into their petal-cups and asked: "Don't you know where little Kay is?"

But every flower stood in the sun, dreaming its own fairy-tale, and Gerda heard many, many of them, but none of them knew anything about Kay.

Here is the tiger-lily's story:

"Do you hear the drum: boom! boom! It has only two notes, always boom! boom! Listen to the women's mourning hymn, hear the priests' call! The Hindu widow stands on the funeral pyre in her long, red sari, the flames leap up around her and her dead husband, but the Hindu woman is thinking of the living man among the watchers, whose eyes burn hotter than the flames, their fire touching her heart more nearly than the flames which are soon to burn her body to ashes. Can the heart's flame die in the flame of the funeral pyre?"

"I don't understand a word of that!" said little Gerda.

"That is my fairy-tale!" said the tiger-lily.

And what did the convolvulus say?

"An ancient castle juts out above the narrow mountain road; dense evergreens climb up the old red walls, leaf by leaf, to the balcony where a beautiful girl stands; she leans out over the balustrade and gazes down the road. No rose branch is fresher than she; no apple blossom when the wind carries it from the tree is as light and airy; how her elegant silken gown rustles! 'Will he never come?'"

"Do you mean Kay?" asked little Gerda.

"I tell only my own story, my own dream," the convolvulus replied.

What did the little daisy say?

"A long plank has been hung on ropes between the trees to make a swing; two sweet little girls, their dresses white as snow, with long green ribbons fluttering from their hats, are swinging while their brother, older than they, stands upright on the swing. He has crooked an arm round one of the ropes to steady himself, because in one hand he holds a little bowl, in the other a clay pipe for blowing bubbles; the swing rises and falls and the bubbles fly, their bright colours changing; the last is still hanging from the pipe, swinging to and fro in the wind; the swing moves up, moves down. The little black dog, light as the bubbles themselves, stands on his hind legs, wishing he were on the

swing; the swing soars, the dog gives up, barking angrily; a soaring swing, a bursting bubble – that is my song!"

"What you say may be very pretty, but you say it sorrowfully, and you never speak of Kay. What do the hyacinths say?"

"There were three lovely sisters, so fragile and fine; one wore a red dress, the second a blue, the third a dress all in white; hand in hand they danced by the calm lake in the bright moonlight. They were not elvish folk, they were human children. The air was filled with fragrance and the girls vanished into the forest; three coffins, in which the three lovely girls lay, glided forth from the wood, and across the lake. Glow-worms flew about them like tiny, hovering lanterns. Are the dancing girls asleep, or are they dead? The fragrance of the flowers says they are dead; the vespers bell rings for the dead!"

"You're making me quite wretched," said little Gerda. "Your scent is so strong it makes me think of the dead girls – oh, is little Kay really dead, then? The roses have been down in the earth and they say he is not!"

"Ding, dong!" rang the hyacinth bells. "We are not ringing for little Kay, we do not know him! We sing our own song, the only one we know."

Gerda went to the buttercup, gleaming among its glossy green leaves.

"You are a bright little sun!" said Gerda. "Tell me, if you know, where I shall find my playmate?"

The buttercup shone back at Gerda: what song could it sing? It was not about Kay.

"God's sun shone warmly down into a little yard on the first day of spring; its beams slid down the neighbour's white walls; nearby, the first yellow flowers grew up, shining gold in the warm rays of the sun; the old grandmother sat out in her chair and her grand-daughter, the poor, pretty servant girl, home on a brief visit, kissed her grandmother. There was gold, her heart's gold in that blessed kiss. Gold in the morning! There, that is my little story!"

"My poor old grandmother!" sighed Gerda. "Yes, she must be missing me, grieving for me just as she did for little Kay. But I shall soon be home again, bringing Kay with me. It's no use asking the flowers, they know nothing but their own songs, they have nothing to tell me!" She hitched up her dress to run, but the narcissus hit her on the leg as she jumped over it. Gerda stopped, staring at the tall, yellow flower, and asked: "Do you know something?" and she stooped towards it. What did the flower say?

"I can see myself, I can see myself!" said the narcissus. "Oh, oh, my scent! Up in the little garret room, half-dressed, is a little dancer; she stands first on one leg, then on both, she kicks out at the whole world, it is all illusion. She pours water from the tea-kettle on to a piece of clothing, her corset – cleanliness is good! Her white dress is hanging on a peg; that too has been washed in the kettle and dried on the roof. She puts it on and winds her saffron-yellow scarf about her neck to make the dress look whiter. Up with her leg! Look how she stands on a single stalk: I can see myself!"

"I don't care a bit about that!" said Gerda, "that is not what I want to hear," and she ran to the far end of the garden.

The door was closed, but she worked at the rusty handle until it gave way, the door sprang open and out went little Gerda on her bare feet, into the wide world. She looked back three times, but no one was following her. At last she could run no more and, when she sat down and looked about her, the summer was over, it was late autumn, only she had never noticed it in the beautiful garden where the sun always shone and there were flowers of all seasons.

"Lord, what a lot of time I have wasted," said little Gerda, "it is autumn now, I dare not rest!" And she got up to go. Her little feet were soon tired and sore, everything looked cold and raw, the long willow leaves were quite yellow and dripping with autumn mist. The leaves fell one by one; only the blackthorn still kept its fruit, bitter enough to pucker your mouth up. Oh, what a grey, gloomy world it was!

THE FOURTH PART

# A prince and a princess

When Gerda had to rest again a big crow landed in the snow just in front of her, looked at her for a long time, cocking its head, and said at last: "Caw, caw! – Hallo, hallo!" That was the best he could do, but he meant it kindly; he asked the little girl where she was going, all alone in the wide world. Gerda understood the word *alone* very well and felt how much it meant, so she told the crow her life story and asked him if he had ever seen Kay.

The crow nodded thoughtfully. "Maybe, maybe," he said.

"What? Have you really?" cried the little girl, almost crushing the crow to death with her kisses.

"Calm down, calm down," said the crow. "I think I know – I think it might be little Kay – but you are forgotten now, for the sake of the princess!"

"Is he living with a princess?" asked Gerda.

20

"He is," said the crow, "but I'm having such trouble speaking your language. If only you understood crow language I could tell it much better!"

"I've never learned it," said Gerda, "but Grandmother spoke it, and she knew *pig Latin* too. If only I had learned it!"

"It doesn't matter," said the crow, "I'll tell you as best I can, but it will still be pretty bad." And he told her all he knew.

"In this kingdom, where we are now, lives a princess who is tremendously clever. She has read all the newspapers in the world and forgotten them again, that's how clever she is! The other day she was sitting on the throne – and that's not much fun either, they say – when she began to hum a tune and found she was singing: 'Why shouldn't I get married?' 'That's not a bad idea,' she said, so she decided to get married. But she wanted a husband who would answer when she spoke to him, not one who just stood about looking distinguished, because that is very boring. She had all her ladies-in-waiting summoned and when they heard what she wanted they were delighted. 'What a good idea!' they said, 'just what I was thinking of myself!' You can believe every word I say," said the crow. "I have a tame sweetheart who moves freely about the castle, and she told me all about it." His sweetheart was a crow, too, of course, for birds of a feather flock together.

All the newspapers were printed with a border of hearts and with the princess's name on them; they announced that any good-looking young man could come to the castle and talk to the princess and the one who talked as if he felt quite at home there, and talked best, was the one the princess would marry. "Yes, yes!" said the crow, "believe me, as sure as I'm standing here, people streamed in, there was such a coming and going, but they had no luck: neither the first day nor the second. They could all talk well while they were out in the street, but as soon as they came through the castle gate and saw the guards in silver and the footmen in gold on the staircase and the great lighted halls,

they were taken aback, and when they reached the throne where the princess sat they could do nothing but repeat the last word she had spoken, and she had no desire to hear that again. Once inside, their tummies seemed to be full of snuff, or they fell into a trance until they were out in the street again, and then, how they talked! The line stretched from the town gates to the castle, I saw it myself!" said the crow. "They got hungry and thirsty, but not so much as a glass of water did they get from the castle. Some of the cleverer ones had brought sandwiches, but they did not share them with their neighbours. They must have thought: 'If he looks hungry, the princess won't take him!'"

"But Kay, little Kay!" cried Gerda. "When did he come? Was he one of the crowd?"

"All in good time! We're just coming to him. It was on the third day that a little fellow arrived, with neither horse nor carriage, marching straight up to the castle, cool as you please. His eyes shone like yours, he had lovely long hair, but his clothes were shabby."

"That was Kay!" cried Gerda joyfully. "Oh, then I've found him!" And she clapped her hands.

"He had a little knapsack on his back," said the crow.

"No, it must have been his sledge," said Gerda, "he went away with a sledge."

"That may well be," said the crow, "I didn't look all that closely. But one thing I know from my tame sweetheart: when he walked through the castle gates and saw the guards in silver and the lackeys in gold all the way up the stairs, he was not a bit dismayed. He gave them a nod and said: 'It must be boring standing on the steps, I'd rather go inside!' The halls were alight with candles, privy counsellors and excellencies walked about in stockinged feet, carrying golden bowls; it was all very ceremonious – and his boots squeaked horribly, yet he wasn't afraid!"

"I'm sure it's Kay," said Gerda, "I know he had new boots, I heard them squeaking in Grandmother's room."

21

"Well, squeak they did," said the crow, "and in he walked, straight up to the princess, who was sitting on a pearl as big as a spinning-wheel, and all the ladies-in-waiting with their maids and their maids' maids, and all the courtiers with their servants and their servants' servants, who kept a lad themselves, drawn up about her. The closer they were to the door, the prouder they looked. The servants' servants' lad, who always wears slippers, was so proud you could scarcely look at him, standing there in the doorway!"

"It must be dreadful," said little Gerda. "But Kay did get the princess?"

"If I hadn't been a crow, I would have taken her, engaged as I am. He seems to have talked as well as I do when I'm speaking crow language, that's what my tame fiancée says. He was cheerful and charming; he said he had not come to court the princess but to listen to her cleverness, and he liked what he heard and she liked him, too."

"Oh, of course it was Kay," said Gerda, "he is so clever that he can do fractions in mental arithmetic! Oh, won't you take me to the castle?"

"That's all very well," said the crow, "but how would we go about it? I'll talk to my tame sweetheart; she may be able to advise us, because I have to tell you that they would never let a little girl like you walk straight in."

"Yes they would," said Gerda. "When Kay hears I am there he will come straight out and fetch me!"

"Wait for me by that stile," said the crow, and with a wag of his head he flew away.

It was dark before the crow returned. "Caw! Caw!" he said, "she sends you many greetings, and here is some bread for you. She took it from the kitchen, where they have bread enough, and you must be hungry. It's impossible for you to enter the castle with your bare feet, the guards in their silver and the lackeys in their gold would not allow it; but don't cry, you'll get there all the same. My sweetheart knows a little back staircase which leads to the bedroom,

and she knows where to find the key."

So they walked down the great avenue, where the leaves were falling one by one, and as the lights were extinguished one by one in the castle, the crow led little Gerda to a back door which was standing ajar.

Oh, how Gerda's heart beat with fear and longing! They were behaving as if she were doing something wrong, yet she only wanted to know if it was little Kay; yes, it must be him; she could see his bright eyes before her now, and his long hair; she could actually see him smiling as he did when they sat at home under the roses. Of course he would be glad to see her, to hear how far she had come for his sake and to know how sad they had been at home when he did not return. Oh, the fear, and the happiness!

They went up the stairs to the first landing, lit by a little lamp set on a cupboard; in the middle of the floor stood the tame crow, cocking her head now this way, now that, and watching Gerda, who curtseyed as her grandmother had taught her.

"My fiancée has said such nice things about you, my little lady," said the tame crow. "Your carriculum vitae, as they call it, is very touching, too! If you will take the lamp, I will walk ahead, down this passage, where we will not meet anyone."

"I think there is someone coming behind us," said Gerda, as something rushed past her; there seemed to be shadows all along the wall, horses with streaming manes and thin legs, huntsmen and ladies and gentlemen on horseback.

"Those are only dreams," said the crow, "come to take their Highnesses' thoughts hunting, fortunately, for you will be the better able to look at them in their beds. But when you come to honour and dignity, I shall expect to see you showing a grateful heart!"

"That's no way to talk," said the forest crow.

They entered the first hall, hung with rose-red satin decorated with artificial flowers; the dreams were rushing past them, so fast that Gerda had no chance to see the royal pair. Each hall was more splendid than the last, an

23

astonishing sight, and then they reached the bedroom. The ceiling of this room was like a great palm tree with leaves of glass, precious glass, and in the middle of the room hung two beds like lilies on a thick golden stalk, one white – that was the princess's bed – and the other red. It was here that Gerda hoped to find little Kay; she turned back one of the red leaves and saw the back of a brown head. Oh, it was Kay! Holding up the lamp she called his name aloud – the dreams rushed back into the room on horseback – he woke up, turned his head, and – it was not Kay.

The prince was like him only from the back, but he was young and handsome. From the white lily bed the princess now looked out and asked what was the matter. Then Gerda cried and told them her whole story and all that the crows had done for her.

"You poor little thing!" said the prince and princess, and they praised the crows and said they were not at all cross with them, though they should not make a habit of it. As it was, they should have a reward. "Do you want to go free?" asked the princess. "Or would you like a permanent post as court crows with all the kitchen leftovers for yourselves?" The two crows bowed and asked for permanent posts, thinking of their old age. "It is very nice to have something for our declining years," as they put it.

The prince got out of his bed and offered it to Gerda – he could scarcely have done more. She folded her little hands and thought, "How good people and animals are, after all," and then she closed her eyes and slept peacefully. All the dreams came flying in again and this time they looked like God's angels, pulling a little sledge, on which sat Kay, nodding to her. But it was only a dream that vanished as soon as she woke up.

The next day she was clothed from head to toe in silk and velvet and invited to stay at the castle and enjoy herself; but all she wanted was

a little horse and carriage, and a pair of boots, so that she could go out into the wide world again to find Kay.

She was given boots and a muff and fine clothes, too, and when she was ready to go a new carriage of pure gold was standing at the door; the coat-of-arms of the prince and princess sparkled on it like a star; coachmen, footmen and outriders – it even had outriders! – wore uniforms made up of golden coins. The prince and princess themselves helped her in to the carriage and wished her good fortune. The forest crow, married now, accompanied her for the first dozen miles or so, sitting beside her because it hated travelling backwards; the other crow stood in the gateway flapping her wings, unable to go because she had had a headache since receiving a permanent post and too much to eat. Inside, the carriage was lined with sugar twists and there were fruit and nuts on the seat.

"Goodbye, goodbye!" called the prince and princess, and little Gerda wept and the crow wept – and so they travelled for the first few miles together. Then the crow too said goodbye, and that was the hardest parting; it flew up into a tree and beat its black wings as long as it could see the carriage, shining like sunlight.

THE FIFTH PART

# *The little robber girl*

They drove through the dark forest, but the brightness of the carriage was like a flame scorching the eyes of certain robbers; it was more than they could stand.

"It's gold, it's gold!" they shouted, and, rushing out and seizing the horses, they killed the little outriders, the coachman and the footmen and dragged Gerda out of the carriage.

"She's fat, she's sweet, she's been fed on nut kernels," said the old robber woman, who had a long, bushy beard and eyebrows that hung down over her eyes. "She's as sweet as a fat little lamb, how good she will taste!" and she drew out her sharp knife, which glinted horribly.

"Ouch!" the old woman cried, as her ear was bitten by her own daughter, who was crouched on her back, as wild and wicked as you please. "Loathsome child!" said her mother, unable to slaughter Gerda.

"She's to play with me!" said the robber girl. "She must give me her muff and her pretty dress and sleep with me in my bed!" And she bit her mother again, so that the old woman leaped in the air and spun round, and all the robbers laughed and shouted: "Look at her dancing with her young 'un!"

"I'm getting into the carriage," said the robber girl, who must and would have her own way, she was so spoiled and stubborn. She and Gerda sat in the carriage and drove through thorn and thicket, deeper and deeper into the forest. The robber girl was no taller than Gerda, but stronger, with broad shoulders and a dark skin; her black eyes had a wistful look. Putting her arms round Gerda, she said: "They shall not kill you, as long as I'm not cross with you. I suppose you're a princess!"

"No," said little Gerda, telling her all her adventures, and how much she loved Kay.

The robber girl stared very solemnly at her and nodded her head gently. "They shall not kill you, even if I do get cross with you – in that case I'll do it myself!" she said. And she dried Gerda's eyes and tucked both her hands inside the pretty muff which was so soft and warm. Then the carriage stopped; they were right inside the courtyard of a robbers' castle. It was split from top to bottom, crows and ravens flew out of the cracks and holes, and the big bulldogs, each massive enough to swallow a man, bounded in the air, but without barking, because that was forbidden.

In the midst of the big, old hall a fire burned on the stone floor, blackening the roof as the smoke rose up and had to make its own way out; a copper cauldron of soup was simmering over it and hares and rabbits were roasting on spits.

"You shall sleep here tonight with me and all my pets," said the robber girl. They were given food and drink and afterwards they went over to a pile of straw and rugs in the corner. Above them were almost a hundred doves, sitting on laths and perches, all apparently sleeping, but they turned their heads a little when the girls arrived.

"They're all mine," said the robber girl, and seizing one of the nearest she held it by the legs and shook it, making it flap its wings. "Kiss it!" she cried, pushing the bird in Gerda's face. "There are the wood-pigeons," she went on, pointing towards a hole with slats fixed across it, high up in the wall. "Those wood-pigeons fly away at once if you don't keep them shut up. And here is my old sweetheart, Bah," and she tugged at the horns of a reindeer which had a bright copper ring round its neck and was tied up.

"We have to keep a tight hold on him, too, or he would run away. Every evening I tickle his neck with my sharp knife to frighten him!" The little girl pulled a long knife from a crack in the wall and let it slide down the reindeer's neck; the unfortunate animal kicked out and the robber girl laughed and pulled Gerda down on the bed with her.

"Do you keep the knife on you when you go to sleep?" asked Gerda, eyeing it nervously.

"I always sleep with a knife," said the robber girl. "You never know what may happen! Now tell me again about Kay and why you went out into the wide world." So Gerda told her story again and the wood-pigeons cooed up

in their cage, while the other doves slept. The robber girl put her arm round Gerda's neck and slept noisily, with the knife in her other hand, but Gerda was unable to close her eyes, wondering whether she was to live or die. The robbers sat round the fire singing and drinking and the old robber woman turned somersaults. Oh, it was a dreadful sight for the little girl to see!

Then the wood-pigeons spoke: "Coo, coo! We have seen little Kay. A white hen was carrying his sledge and he was sitting in the Snow Queen's carriage as she flew low over the forest where we were sitting on our nests; she blew on us fledglings and they all died except for us. Coo, coo!"

"What are you saying up there?" cried Gerda, "where was the Snow Queen going? Have you any idea?"

"She must have been going to Lapland, where there is always snow and ice. Ask that reindeer tied up down there."

"A place with snow and ice is a good and blessed place," said the reindeer, "where you can run free in the great, shining valleys where the Snow Queen has her summer tent. But her real castle is up near the North Pole, on the island called Spitsbergen."

"Oh Kay, little Kay!" sighed Gerda.

"Lie still now," said the robber girl, "or you'll get my knife in your stomach!"

In the morning Gerda told her what the wood-pigeons had said about Kay and the robber girl looked very serious, but she nodded and said: "It's the right one, it's the right one! Do you know where Lapland is?" she asked the reindeer.

"Who should know better than I?" said the creature, his eyes rolling in his head. "I was born and bred there, I ran across the snowfields there."

"Listen," the robber girl told Gerda, "you can see that all our menfolk are out. Mother is still here and she will stay, but later in the morning she'll have a drink from the big bottle and take a little nap; then I'll do something for you!"

She jumped off the bed, ran and flung her

arms round her mother, pulled her beard and said: "My own sweet billygoat, good morning!" And her mother tweaked her nose so that it turned red and blue, but it was all done for love. After her mother had drunk from the bottle and was taking a little nap, the robber girl told the reindeer: "I would have loved to go on tickling you many more times with my sharp knife, because you're so funny, but never mind. Now I'm going to untie you and help you get out so that you can run to Lapland, but you must make haste and carry this little girl to the Snow Queen's palace where her playmate is. You heard what she said, because she was talking quite loudly and you were listening!"

The reindeer leaped for joy. The robber girl hoisted little Gerda on to its back and took the precaution of tying her fast and even giving her a little cushion to sit on. "I suppose I might as well let you have your fleecy boots," she said, "because it will be cold, but I'm going to keep the muff, it's so sweet! All the same, you mustn't freeze. Here are my mother's big mittens, they'll come up to your elbows; put your hands in!

Now your hands look just like my ugly old mother's!"

Gerda wept for joy.

"I can't bear you whining!" said the robber girl. "You're supposed to look pleased! Here are two loaves and a ham for you, so that you won't starve." Loaves and ham were tied on the reindeer's back; the robber girl opened the door, called all the big dogs in and cut the reindeer's rope with her knife. "Run along," she told it, "but take good care of the little girl!"

Gerda stretched out her hands in their big mittens to the robber girl and said goodbye. Then the reindeer flew off over bushes and shrubs, through the great forest, across marshes and plains, as fast as it could go. The wolves howled, the ravens shrieked, and "Tshoo! tshoo!" said the sky, just as if it were sneezing red.

"There are my old Northern Lights!" said the reindeer, "see how bright they are!" And on it ran, faster still, by night and day; the loaves were eaten up, and so was the ham, and then they were in Lapland.

THE SIXTH PART

# The Lapp woman and the Finnish woman

They stopped by a little house, a wretched place, with a roof which reached to the ground and a doorway so low that the family had to wriggle through on their stomachs when they wanted to go in or out. No one was in but an old Lapp woman, standing over an oil-lamp, frying fish. The reindeer told her Gerda's story, but first he told her his own, which he thought far more important, and Gerda was so overcome with cold that she could not even speak.

"Oh, you poor things," said the Lapp woman, "you have a long way to go yet. It is over a hundred miles from here to Finmark, where the Snow Queen is on holiday, lighting

fireworks every single night. I'll write a note for you on a dried cod – I have no paper – and you can take it to the Finnish woman up there, who can advise you better than I can!"

As Gerda was warm now and had had something to eat and drink, the Lapp woman wrote a few words on a dried codfish, told Gerda to take good care of it, tied her firmly on the reindeer again, and off it ran.

"Tshoo! Tshoo!" went the sky, where the beautiful blue Northern Lights burned all night long. When they came to Finmark they knocked on the Finnish woman's chimney, for she did not even have a door. It was so hot inside that

the Finnish woman herself, short and rather dirty, went about almost naked. She unbuttoned Gerda's clothes at once, took off her mittens and boots so that she would not be too hot, laid a piece of ice on the reindeer's head and then read what was written on the codfish. When she had read it three times through, she knew it by heart and could put the fish in the pot, for it was good to eat and she never wasted anything.

The reindeer told his story first and then Gerda's, and the Finnish woman narrowed her intelligent eyes, but said nothing.

"You are so clever," said the reindeer, "I know you can bind all the winds of the world on a piece of thread; if the sailor unties the first knot he gets a good wind, if he unties the second, he gets a strong blow and if he unties the third and fourth knots there is a storm, a wind to blow forests down! Won't you let this little girl have a potion which will give her the strength of twelve, to defeat the Snow Queen?"

"The strength of twelve," said the Finnish woman, "yes, that should be enough!" and from a shelf she took a large roll of skin, and unrolled it. Curious letters were inscribed on it, which the Finnish woman read until the drops

fell like rain from her forehead. But the reindeer begged her again to do something for little Gerda and Gerda looked at her with such pleading eyes, filled with tears, that the Finnish woman herself began to blink. She drew the reindeer into a corner, where she applied fresh ice to its head and whispered: "Little Kay really is with the Snow Queen, and he is very happy there. He firmly believes it's the best place in the world, but that's because he has a splinter of glass in his heart and a speck of glass in his eye; they must go first, otherwise he will never come to manhood and the Snow Queen will keep her power over him."

"But can't you give Gerda enough power to do that?"

"I can't give her more power than she already has! Don't you see how great it is, how people and animals have to serve her, or how could she have come so far on her bare feet? She must not learn of her power from us; it lies in her heart, it lies in her being a sweet, innocent child. If she herself cannot reach the Snow Queen and take the glass from Kay's heart, we cannot help. Ten miles from here the Snow Queen's gardens begin and that far you can carry the little girl yourself; put her down by the big bush which bears red berries in the snow, don't stand about chattering, but hurry back here!'' Then the Finnish woman lifted little Gerda on to the reindeer, which ran off as fast as it could go.

"Oh, I haven't got my boots, I haven't got my mittens!'' cried Gerda, feeling the stinging cold, but the reindeer dared not stop, it ran until it reached the bush with the red berries, where it put Gerda down and kissed her on the lips, great shining tears running down its cheeks. Then it ran off again, as hard as it could, back the way it had come. There stood poor Gerda, with neither shoes nor gloves, in the terrible, icy cold of Finmark.

Running on as fast as she could go, she was met by a whole regiment of snowflakes; but these had not fallen from the sky, which was quite clear, and brilliant with Northern Lights; the snowflakes moved along close to the ground, and the closer they came, the bigger they grew. Gerda remembered how big and strange the snowflakes had looked through a magnifying glass, but these were big and terrible in quite a different way, they were alive, they were the outposts of the Snow Queen. Their shapes were extraordinary, some were like big, ugly hedge-hogs, others like bunches of snakes poking their heads out, and yet others like fat little bears, every hair on end, all shining white, all living snowflakes.

Then little Gerda said the Lord's Prayer aloud, her breath hanging in the cold, cold air like smoke, growing more and more dense, until it took the form of bright little angels, which grew taller as they touched the ground. Each wore a helmet and carried a shield and spear; their numbers grew until, as Gerda reached the end of her prayer, she was surrounded by a whole legion of angels, who flung their spears at the horrid snowflakes, which shattered into a hundred fragments, and Gerda was safe and sound again. When the angels patted her feet and hands they felt less cold and she walked quickly on towards the Snow Queen's palace.

But now we must see what is happening to Kay. He was not thinking about little Gerda at all, and least of all that she was already standing outside the palace gate.

THE SEVENTH PART

# *What happened in the Snow Queen's palace and what happened afterwards*

The walls of the palace were built of snowdrifts and the windows and doors were made by the piercing winds; there were over a hundred rooms, according to where the snow had drifted, and the biggest were many miles long. Each one was lit by the bright Northern Lights, each one was very big, very empty, brilliant and icy-cold. There was no merriment here, not even so much as a little bears' party, where the storm winds could blow and the polar bears walk on their hind legs and show off their manners; never a little game of cards with a snack to eat and polite conversation; never a nice little coffee party for the white lady foxes: empty, big and cold – that was all you could say for the Snow Queen's halls. The Northern

Lights blazed so regularly that you could tell when they were at their highest and when at their lowest. Right in the middle of the empty, endless halls of snow there was a frozen lake, cracked in a thousand pieces, but the pieces matched so perfectly that they made a real picture puzzle. In the middle of it sat the Snow Queen, when she was at home, and she liked to say that she was sitting in the mirror of reason, the best, the only one in all the world.

Little Kay was quite blue with cold – almost black, in fact – but he had not noticed, for she had kissed the cold shuddering out of him and his heart was little more than a lump of ice. He was pushing some of the jagged, flat pieces of ice about, arranging them in all kinds of patterns, trying to make something. To us it would have been like the little bits of wood we fit into a jig-saw puzzle. Kay was making patterns too, the strangest you ever saw, in his icy game of reason; in his eyes the patterns were quite remarkable and of the greatest possible import-ance, because of the speck of glass in his eye. He was arranging the pieces into words, but he could never manage to make the word he wanted, the word *eternity*. The Snow Queen had said: "If you can discover that pattern, you shall be your own master and I shall give you the whole world and a new pair of skates." But he could not.

"Now I am rushing off to the warm countries," the Snow Queen told him, "I want to have a look inside the black cauldrons!" She meant the fire-spouting volcanoes, Etna and Vesuvius, as we call them. "I must whiten them a little, that's right and proper, and it will go well with the lemons and grapes!" Off she flew, leaving Kay all alone in the mile-long, empty hall of ice, looking at the fragments and think-ing and thinking, until the thoughts gnawed at his brain; so stiff and still he sat that you would have thought he had frozen to death.

Then it was that little Gerda walked into the palace through the great doorway of tearing wind; but she said her evening prayer and the wind was hushed as if it had fallen asleep. So she stepped into the great, empty, chilly hall – and saw Kay. She recognized him, threw her arms round him, hugged him tight and cried: "Kay! Dear Kay! I've found you at last!"

But he sat quite still, stiff and cold, and little Gerda shed hot tears which fell upon his breast. They pierced him to the heart, thawing the lump of ice and melting the little splinter of glass inside it; he looked at her and she sang their old hymn:

"In the valley roses grow,
There the Christ-child we shall know!"

Kay burst into tears and cried until the speck of glass was washed from his eye; then he recognized Gerda and gave a joyful cry: "Gerda! Dear Gerda! Where have you been all this time, and where have I been?" He looked about him. "How cold it is, how big and empty it is here!" He clung to Gerda and she laughed and cried with happiness; it was such a blessed moment that even the ice fragments danced for joy and when they were tired they lay down again and formed the very word the Snow Queen had told him to make in order to be his own master and receive the whole world and a new pair of skates.

Gerda kissed his cheeks and they grew rosy again; she kissed his eyes and they shone like her own; she kissed his hands and feet and he was fit and healthy again. The Snow Queen could return when she liked, his pass was written there in shining fragments of ice.

Hand in hand they left the great palace, talk-ing of Grandmother and of the roses on the roof, and, where they walked, the winds were hushed and the sun broke through. When they reached the bush with the red berries the reindeer was waiting for them, with another young reindeer, a doe with full udders, from which she gave the children warm milk to drink. The two reindeer kissed Kay and Gerda and carried them first to the Finnish woman, where they warmed them-selves in her hot cabin and were given instruc-tions for the journey home, and then to the

Lapp woman, who had made them new clothes and prepared her sledge for them.

The reindeer and the young doe ran alongside as far as the borders of the country, where the first green leaves were showing, and there they all said goodbye.

The first small birds were beginning to twitter, the trees bore green buds and, from among them, on a splendid horse which Gerda knew, for it had been harnessed to the golden carriage, rode a girl who wore a bright red cap on her head and had two pistols stuck in her belt. It was the little robber girl, who was tired of staying at home and had decided to travel, first north and then, if she was not enjoying herself, in some other direction. She recognized Gerda at once, and Gerda recognized her – how happy they were!

"You're a fine one for gadding about!" she told Kay. "I wonder if you deserve to have people running to the ends of the earth for your sake?"

But Gerda patted her cheek and asked about the prince and princess.

"They are travelling in foreign lands!" said the robber girl.

"And the crow?" asked little Gerda.

"Ah, the crow is dead," she replied. "His tame sweetheart is a widow and wears a bit of black wool tied round her leg; she makes a great fuss, whining and complaining, and it's all a lot of rubbish! But now tell me what has been happening to you, and how you found him."

So Gerda and Kay told her together.

"So all's well that ends well!" said the robber girl, and taking both their hands she promised to come and see them if ever she passed through their town. Then she rode off into the wide world.

But Kay and Gerda walked on, hand in hand, and wherever they walked it was springtime. Flowers and green leaves were everywhere, the church bells were ringing, and they recognized the tall towers of the big town where they lived. Passing in, they walked up to the door of Grandmother's house, up the stairs, into the room where everything still stood where it always had, and the clock said: "Tick-tock!" and the hands moved. But as they passed through the door they noticed that they had become grown-up people.

The roses in the window boxes were growing in through the open window and the two children's chairs were standing there, so Kay and Gerda sat, each on their own chair, still holding hands; the cold, empty splendour of the Snow Queen's palace was forgotten like a bad dream. Grandmother was sitting in God's bright sunshine, reading aloud from the Bible: "Except ye become as little children, ye shall not enter into the kingdom of heaven!"

Kay and Gerda looked into each other's eyes and all at once they understood their old hymn:

"In the valley roses grow:
There the Christ-child we shall know!"

There they sat, grown-up and yet still children, children at heart, and it was summer, the warm, wonderful summer.

# The Goblin and the Grocer

Once upon a time there was a proper student, who lived in the attic and owned nothing; once upon a time there was a proper grocer, who lived on the ground floor and owned the whole house and the goblin attached himself to the grocer, for there, every Christmas Eve, he received a bowl of porridge with a big lump of butter on it. The grocer was rich enough to give him it, so the goblin stayed in the shop and there's a lesson to be learned from that.

One evening the student came in at the back door to buy candles and cheese. Having no one to send, he came himself, was given what he asked for, paid for it, received a nodded "Good evening," from the grocer and his lady – and there was a woman who could do more than nod, she really had the gift of the gab! – and the student nodded back and stood where he was, reading the piece of paper which had been wrapped round the cheese. It was a page torn from an old book which should not have been torn to pieces, an old book full of poetry.

"There's more of it," said the grocer, "I gave an old woman some coffee beans for it; if you pay me eight pence, you shall have the rest."

"Thank you," said the student, "but you can let me have it instead of the cheese. I can eat plain bread and butter and it would be a shame if the whole of that book were to be torn to bits and pieces. You are a fine man and a practical man, but you have no more understanding of poetry than that bin there."

What he said was rude, especially to the bin, but the grocer laughed and the student laughed – after all, he had said it as a kind of joke. But the goblin was annoyed to hear someone speaking to a grocer in that fashion – a grocer who was a landlord and sold the best butter!

When it was night, with the shop locked and everyone in bed except the student, the goblin went in and took madam's gift of the gab, which she did not need while she was asleep. Whatever object he laid it on received the power of speech and could express its thoughts and feelings just as well as madam herself. Only one at a time could have it, however, and that was a blessing, for otherwise they would all have been talking at once.

So the goblin gave the gift of the gab to the bin containing the old newspapers: "Is it really true," he asked, "that you don't know what poetry is?"

"Oh, but I do," said the bin, "it's one of those things they put at the end of the newspaper that gets cut out; I should think I have more of it in me than the student, and I am only a poor bin, compared to the grocer."

Then the goblin put the gift of the gab on the coffee mill, and oh, how it turned! And he put it on the butter churn and on the till and all of them thought as the bin did, and what the majority agree on must be respected.

"Now for the student!" said the goblin, stealing up the kitchen stairs to the attic where the student lived. There was a light inside and when the goblin peeped through the keyhole he saw the student reading the tattered book from the shop. But how light it was in there! A clear

beam of light shone from the book and grew into a trunk, into a mighty tree which rose up and spread its broad green branches above the student. Every leaf was fresh and green, every flower a sweet girl's face, some with eyes that were dark and shining, while others were blue and extraordinarily clear. Every fruit was a shining star and from the tree came a wonderful sound of singing.

Well, the little goblin had never imagined, let alone seen and heard such splendours and he went on standing there on tiptoe, gazing and gazing until the light inside went out. The student had blown out his oil lamp and gone to bed, but the little goblin stayed where he was, because he could still hear the sweet sound of the song in his ears, a lovely lullaby for the student as he went to sleep.

"This is extraordinary!" said the little goblin, "I was not expecting anything like it – and I think I shall stay with the student after all." Then he thought again – and he used his commonsense and sighed – and back he went to the grocer. It was a good thing that he did, for the bin had used up almost all madam's gift of the gab by declaring from one side everything it had in it and it was just turning round to repeat it all from the other side, when the goblin came in and returned the gift of the gab to madam. But, from that time on, the whole shop, from the cash till to the kindling stack, thought as the bin did and they respected it so much and had so much faith in it that when the grocer read out the "Art and Theatre News" from his newspaper in the evening they thought it all came from the bin.

But the little goblin no longer sat peacefully listening to all that wisdom and good sense down below. As soon as a light shone out from the attic room its beams seemed like strong anchor cables pulling him upward and he had to go and peep in through the keyhole until there arose within him the kind of greatness we feel by the rolling sea when God passes over it in the storm winds. The little goblin burst into tears. He himself had no idea why he was weep-

ing, but there was something good in his tears. How uniquely wonderful it must be to sit under the tree with the student! But, as it could not be done, he was glad of the keyhole. There he stood, on and on in the cold passageway, while the autumn winds blew down through the trap-door in the loft and it was very, very cold, but the little goblin did not feel the cold until the light went out in the garret and the wind drowned the music within. Whoo! Then he began to freeze and crept down again to his warm corner – how cosy and comfortable it was! – and when the Christmas porridge arrived with a big lump of butter on it, well, the grocer was his master after all.

Poor goblin – in the middle of the night he was awakened by a fearful banging on the shutters and a commotion outside. The night-watchman's whistle sounded "Fire!" The whole street was lit by the glare. Was it in this house or the neighbour's? Where? This was terrible! The grocer's lady was so flustered that she took off her gold earrings and put them in her pocket in order to save something from the fire, the grocer ran for his bonds and the serving-girl for the silk mantilla which she had managed to buy for herself; everyone wanted to save the best he had, and so did the little goblin. In two bounds he was up the stairs and in the attic of the student, who was standing calmly by the open window watching the fire in the neigh-bour's yard. The little goblin grabbed the miraculous book from the table, popped it in his red cap and held on to it with both hands: the treasure of the house was saved! Then off he rushed, up to the roof, and on top of the chimney, and there he sat, lit by the burning house next door, clutching with both hands the red cap in which the treasure lay. Now he knew his own heart and to whom he really belonged, but, when the fire had been put out and he returned to his senses – well: "I'll divide myself between them!" he said, "I can't just let the grocer go, for the sake of the porridge!"

That was entirely human: the rest of us go to the grocer, too – for porridge.

# Little Claus and Big Claus

Once upon a time there were two men who lived in the same village and had the same name. They were both called Claus, but one of them owned four horses and the other only one horse, so, in order to distinguish them, the one who had four horses was known as Big Claus and the one who had only one horse, Little Claus. Now we are going to hear what happened to them, for this is a true story.

All through the week Little Claus had to plough for Big Claus and lend him his one horse. Then Big Claus would help him with all four of his horses, but only once a week, and that was on Sunday.

"Gee up!" Little Claus would crack his whip over all five horses which were as good as his for that one day. The sun shone brightly and all the bells in the church tower rang for church. The people wore their Sunday best and walked along with their hymn books under their arms to hear the preacher preaching. They saw Little Claus ploughing with five horses and he was so delighted that he cracked his whip again and cried: "Gee up, all my horses!"

"You must not say that!" said Big Claus, "only one of the horses is yours."

But when someone else passed by on his way to church Little Claus forgot that he was not allowed to shout: "Gee up, all my horses!"

"Now I am going to appeal to you to stop," said Big Claus, "and if you say that one more time I shall hit your horse on the head so hard that it dies on the spot and you will have no horse left."

"I really won't say it again," said Little Claus, but when some more people passed and nodded good morning to him, he was so pleased with himself and thought he looked so dashing with five horses to plough his land that he cracked his whip and shouted again: "Gee up, all my horses!"

"I'll gee up your horses!" said Big Claus and, picking up the mallet he used for his cattle stakes, he hit Little Claus's one horse on the head with it and the horse fell down, quite dead.

"Oh, now I have no horse at all!" said Little Claus and he began to cry. Then he skinned the horse and dried the skin thoroughly in the wind, put it in a bag which he hung round his neck and went into the town to sell his horse's hide.

His long walk took him through a big, dark wood, and the weather suddenly turned very nasty. He got completely lost and, before he found the road again, it was evening and much too far for him to reach the town or return home before nightfall.

Close to the road lay a big farmhouse. Its window-shutters were closed, but light still

shone out above the shutters. "I could ask them to let me stay the night there," thought Little Claus, and he knocked at the door.

The farmer's wife opened it, but when she heard his request she said he must be on his way because her husband was not at home and she did not take in strangers.

"Oh well, I shall have to sleep outside then," said Little Claus, and the farmer's wife locked the door.

Close by there was a big haystack and between it and the house stood a little shed with a flat thatched roof.

"I could lie on that," said Little Claus, "that will make a fine bed, and I'm sure the stork won't fly down and bite my legs." (There was a real live stork on its nest on the rooftop above him.)

Little Claus climbed on top of the shed, where he lay down and turned over to find a comfortable position. The wooden shutters at the windows did not reach right to the top so that he could see straight into the room. There was a big table ready laid, with wine and roast meat and a fine fish as well. The farmer's wife and the deacon were sitting at the table, and there was no one else there at all. She poured out for him and he dug into the fish, because he was very fond of it.

"If only I could have some too!" said Little Claus, leaning out towards the window. Heavens, what a wonderful cake he could see in there – it was a real feast!

Then he heard someone riding down the road towards the house. It was the farmer's wife's husband, coming home.

Now the farmer was a good man, but he suffered from one strange complaint: he could not stand the sight of deacons. As soon as a deacon came into view he would fly into a rage. That was the reason why the deacon had gone in to visit the farmer's wife when he knew that her husband was not at home and that was also why the good woman had set out the most delicious meal she could for him. As soon as they heard her husband coming they were thoroughly scared and the farmer's wife told the deacon to crawl inside a big, empty chest in the corner of the room. The deacon did so, because he knew very well that her poor husband could not stand the sight of deacons. The woman hastily hid all the delicious food and wine in her baking oven, because if her husband had set eyes on it he would have wanted to know what was going on.

"Oh dear!" sighed Little Claus on top of the shed, as he saw all the food disappearing.

"Is there someone up there?" asked the farmer, and he looked up and saw Little Claus. "Why are you lying there? You come on inside with me!"

So Little Claus told him how he had got lost and asked if he could stay the night.

"Of course!" said the farmer, "but first we need a spot of food."

The wife welcomed them both very kindly,

40

set out a long table and gave them each a big bowl of porridge. The farmer was hungry and ate with a good appetite, but Little Claus could not stop thinking about the delicious roast meat, fish and cake which he knew were in the oven. He had put his sack containing the horse's hide under the table at his feet, for, as we know, he had left home in order to sell it in the town. He simply could not get the porridge down, so he gave his bag a push and the dry skin in the sack creaked aloud.

"Hush!" said Little Claus to his sack, but he gave it another push and it squeaked even louder than before.

"What on earth have you got in your bag?" asked the farmer.

"Oh, it's just a wizard," said Little Claus. "He says there is no need for us to eat porridge because he has filled the oven with meat and fish and cake by magic."

"What's this!" said the farmer and hastening to open the oven he saw all the delicious food his wife had hidden, but which he now believed the wizard in the sack had put there by magic. The woman dared not speak, but laid the food on the table and the two of them ate fish and roast meat and cake together. Then Little Claus pressed the bag with his foot again, making the hide squeak.

"What does he say now?"

"He says," said Little Claus, "that he has also produced three bottles of wine for us by magic, over in the corner by the stove." So the woman had to take out the wine she had hidden and the farmer drank it and became very merry. He would dearly have loved to own a wizard like the one Little Claus had in his sack.

"Can he conjure up the devil by magic too?" asked the farmer. "I'd like to see him, now that I'm so merry!"

"Yes," said Little Claus, "my wizard can do anything I wish. Isn't that so?" he asked, stepping on the bag, which squeaked again. "Did you hear him saying yes? But the devil is so ugly that it's better not to see him."

"Oh I'm not a bit frightened. What do you think he looks like?"

"Well, he'll look like a real, live deacon!"

"Huh!" said the farmer, "that is ugly. I'd better tell you that I can't stand the sight of deacons, but no matter, now I know it's the devil, I'll be able to put up with it. I've got some courage now, but he mustn't come too near me."

"I'm going to ask my wizard," said Little Claus, and he stepped on the bag and put a hand to his ear.

"What does he say?"

"He says that if you go and open the chest in the corner you will see the devil squatting in there, but you must hold on to the lid so that he doesn't escape!"

"Would you help me to hold it?" said the farmer, going over to the chest where his wife had hidden the real deacon, who was now very frightened.

The farmer lifted the lid a little way and peered in under it. "Oooh!" he yelled, jumping back. "Yes, I've seen him now, he looked exactly like our deacon. Oh, that was terrible."

They needed a drink after that and they went on drinking late into the night.

"You must sell me that wizard," said the farmer. "Ask what you like for him. I'll give you a whole bushelful of money right away."

"No, I can't do that," said Little Claus, "just think of all the gifts I can get from that wizard!"

"Oh, I did want it so much," said the farmer, and he started pleading.

"All right," said Little Claus at last, "you've been so kind and given me shelter for the night, so I'll give in. You shall have the wizard for a bushelful of money, but you must fill the bushel right to the top."

"You shall have it," said the farmer, "but you must take that chest over there with you, I don't want to have it in the house an hour longer. You never know, he might still be in there."

Little Claus gave the farmer his sack with the dry hide in it and was given a bushelful of money, and filled right to the top at that. The

farmer also presented him with a big wheel-barrow to cart the money and the chest away.

"Goodbye!" said Little Claus and off he went with the money and the big chest with the deacon still sitting inside it.

On the far side of the wood ran a broad, deep river. The current was so strong that it was almost impossible to swim against it; a fine new bridge had been built across it and in the very middle of the bridge Little Claus stopped and said aloud, so that the deacon could hear him:

"Now what do I want with this wretched chest? It's as heavy as if it were filled with stones. I'm getting worn out pushing it, so I'll throw it in the river. That way it will sail home to me on its own if it likes and if it doesn't, no matter."

He gripped the chest with one hand and lifted it a little as if he were about to push it into the water.

"No, stop!" cried the deacon inside the chest, "you must let me out!"

"Oooh!" said Little Claus, pretending to be frightened. "He's still in there, I must get it in the river quickly and drown him."

"Oh no, oh no!" cried the deacon, "I'll give you a bushelful of money if you don't."

"Well, that's a different matter," said Little Claus, opening the chest. The deacon scrambled out, pushed the empty chest into the water and went home, where he gave Little Claus a bushelful of money. Since he had already been given one bushel by the farmer, the wheel-barrow was now completely full of money.

"I did very well selling that horse, I must say!" he said to himself, when he returned home and tipped all the money in a big heap on the floor. "It will annoy Big Claus when he hears how rich I've got with my one horse, but I'm not going to go and tell him straight out."

So he sent a boy over to Big Claus to borrow a bushel measure.

"What does he want with that?" thought Big Claus, and he smeared some tar in the bottom of the measure to catch a little of the goods being measured. His trick worked: when the bushel came back there were three new silver shillings stuck inside it.

"What's this?" said Big Claus and he ran over to see Little Claus. "Where did you get all that money from?"

"Oh, I got it for my horse's hide. I sold it last night."

"You certainly did well with that," said Big Claus, and running home to fetch an axe, he hit all four of his horses on the head, took off

44

their skins and drove into town with them.

"Hides, hides, hides for sale!" he shouted all along the streets.

All the shoemakers and tanners came running out to ask what he wanted for them.

"A bushel of money for each," said Big Claus.

"Are you mad?" said they, "do you think we have money by the bushel?"

"Hides, hides, hides for sale!" he shouted again, but to all those who asked the price of the hides he replied: "A bushelful of coins."

"He's trying to make a fool of us," said they, and the cobblers took their straps and the tanners their leather aprons and began to beat Big Claus.

"Hides, hides!" they scoffed, "yes, we'll give you a hiding right enough. Chase him out of town!" they shouted, and Big Claus had to run with all his might to escape the worst beating he had ever had.

"Ha," he said, when he got home, "Little Claus will pay for this, I'll kill him for this!"

But Little Claus had come home to find his old grandmother dead. She had certainly been bad-tempered and unkind to him, yet he was quite upset, and picking up the dead woman he laid her in his own warm bed as if she might come to life again. She should lie there all night and he would sleep on a chair in the corner – it would not be the first time.

During the night the door opened and Big Claus came in with his axe. He knew very well where Little Claus's bed stood and he went straight to it and struck the dead grandmother on the head, believing her to be Little Claus.

"There!" he said, "you won't make a fool of me again!" and he went home.

"That's a bad, wicked man," said Little Claus, "he was trying to kill me and it's a good thing my old grandmother was dead already or he would have killed her."

He dressed his old grandmother in her Sunday clothes, borrowed a horse from his neighbour, harnessed it to the cart, settled his grandmother on the back seat so that she would not fall out as he drove along and off they went through the woods. When the sun came up they stopped outside a big inn, where Little Claus went in for a bite to eat.

The innkeeper had a great deal of money and although he was a very good man he was hot-tempered, as if he were stuffed with pepper and tobacco.

"Good morning!" he said to Little Claus, "you're out very early today, in your smart town clothes!"

"Yes," said Little Claus, "I'm going into town with my old grandmother. She's out there in the cart, I can't get her to come inside. Would you take her a glass of mead, but you will have to speak very loudly, her hearing is not too good."

"Yes, I'll do that," said the innkeeper, pouring out a glass of mead which he took out to the dead grandmother, sitting propped up in the cart.

"Here is a glass of mead from your grandson," said the innkeeper, but the dead woman said not a word.

"Can't you hear me?" shouted the innkeeper as loud as he could: "Here's a glass of mead from your grandson!"

He shouted his message again and then again, but when she did not stir he grew angry and threw the glass in her face so that the mead ran down her nose and she fell backwards into the cart, because she was only propped up and not tied fast.

"What's this?" cried Little Claus, running out and seizing the innkeeper by his shirt-front. "You've gone and killed my grandmother! Just look, there's a big hole in her forehead."

"Oh, what a disaster!" cried the innkeeper, beating his hands together, "it's all because of my bad temper. Dear Little Claus, I will give you a whole bushelful of money and have your grandmother buried as if she were my own, if only you will keep quiet, otherwise they will chop my head off and that's very nasty."

So Little Claus got a whole bushelful of money and the innkeeper buried his old grandmother as if she had been his own.

As soon as Little Claus came home again with all his money he sent his boy over to Big Claus to borrow a bushel measure.

"What's this?" asked Big Claus, "didn't I kill him? I must look into this myself." So he took the bushel over to Little Claus himself.

"Well, where did you get all that money from?" he asked, his eyes popping at the sight of yet another pile of money.

"It was my grandmother, not me you killed," said Little Claus, "so I sold her and got a bushelful of money for her."

"You did well out of it," said Big Claus, and hurrying home he took an axe and killed his old grandmother, put her in his cart, drove into town where the apothecary lived and asked if he wanted to buy a dead body.

"Who is it and where did you get it from?" asked the apothecary.

"It's my grandmother," said Big Claus, "I

killed her for a bushelful of money."

"God save us!" said the apothecary. "You've given yourself away now, don't say things like that or you'll lose your head!"

He explained to Big Claus what a terribly wicked thing he had done and what kind of man he was and that he deserved to be punished. Big Claus was so terrified that he ran straight out of the apothecary's shop to his cart, whipped up the horses and drove home. But the apothecary and all the people thought he was mad and they let him go where he liked.

"I'll pay you out for this!" said Big Claus, when he was on the country road, "oh yes, I'll pay you out, Little Claus!" And as soon as he got home he found his biggest sack, went over to Little Claus and said: "Now you have fooled me again, first I killed my horses, then my old grandmother. It's all your fault but you will never fool me again." And seizing Little Claus, he pushed him into the sack, picked him up by the neck and shouted: "Now I'm going to drown you!"

It was a long walk to the river and Little Claus was not a light weight to carry. The road led past the church where the organ was playing and the people were singing inside. Big Claus put down the sack with Little Claus inside it at the church door, thinking that it would be a good idea to go in and listen to a hymn first before he went on; Little Claus could not escape and all the people were in church, so he went inside.

"Oh dear, oh dear!" sighed Little Claus inside the sack. He twisted and turned but could not free himself. At that moment an old herdsman with snow-white hair, carrying a big crook in his hand, came driving a herd of cows and bulls along the road; they bumped into the sack and it overturned with Little Claus inside it.

"Oh dear!" sighed Little Claus, "I am so young, and yet I must go to heaven."

"And poor old me!" said the herdsman, "old as I am, I can't get there yet."

"Open the sack!" cried Little Claus, "crawl inside in my place and you'll go straight to heaven!"

"I'd like that very much," said the herdsman, and he untied Little Claus who jumped out straight away.

"Will you keep an eye on the cattle?" said the old man, crawling inside the sack, which Little Claus tied up again before he moved on, driving all the cows and bulls ahead of him.

Soon afterwards Big Claus came out of the church and picked up the sack again, thinking how light it was now, for the old herdsman weighed no more than half as much as Little Claus. "How light he is to carry now, it must be because I have been listening to a hymn!" and on he walked to the river, which was deep and wide, and throwing the sack with the old herdsman inside it into the water he shouted, thinking he was talking to Little Claus: "There! You'll never make a fool of me again!"

Then he went home, but when he reached the crossroads he met Little Claus driving all his cattle home.

"What's this! Didn't I drown you?"

"Oh yes!" said Little Claus, "you threw me in the river not half an hour ago."

"But where did you get all those fine cattle from?" asked Big Claus.

"They are river cattle," said Little Claus, "I'll tell you the whole story, and I give you my thanks, too, for drowning me, now that I'm out again. I'm really rich now, believe me! I was very frightened when I was in the sack and the wind howled round my ears when you threw me off the bridge into the cold water. I sank straight to the bottom, but I didn't hurt myself because I fell on the lovely soft grass that grows down there. The sack was immediately opened by a beautiful girl in a white dress, who wore a green wreath on her wet hair. She took my hand and said: 'So it's you, Little Claus? Here are some cattle for you and five miles up the road you will find a whole herd, which I am going to give you!' Then I saw that the river was like a big road for the water people. Along the bottom the people were walking and driving in from the sea, right across the country to where

the river ends. It was a beautiful place, full of flowers and fresh grass and fish swimming in the water, which flitted past my ears as the birds of the air do here. What beautiful people they were and what a lot of cattle, walking along the hedges and ditches."

"But why did you come straight back here?" asked Big Claus. "I wouldn't have done that, if it was so wonderful down there."

"Well," said Little Claus, "that was just my cunning. You heard me tell you that the water girl said there was a whole herd of cattle waiting for me five miles up the road – and by road she meant river, because that was the only place she knew. But I know that the river bends, now this way, now that, and you can take a short cut by coming up on land and walking across to meet the river again. It will save me about two miles and I'll reach my water cattle all the sooner."

"Oh, you are a lucky man," said Big Claus, "do you think I would get some water-cattle too, if I went to the bottom of the river?"

"Yes, I should think so," said Little Claus, "but I can't carry you to the river in a sack, you are too heavy for me. If you like to walk there

on your own feet and then crawl into the sack, I'll push you over with the greatest of pleasure.

"Thank you very much!" said Big Claus, "but if I don't get any water-cattle when I get there you can be sure of a beating."

"Oh no, don't be so unkind!" said Little Claus.

Off they walked to the river, where the cattle, which were thirsty, ran as fast as they could to have a drink.

"See them running!" said Little Claus, "they want to get back to the bottom of the river again."

"Well, help me first," said Big Claus, "or else I'll beat you!" And he clambered into a big sack which had been lying across the back of one of the bulls. "Put a stone in it, otherwise I'm afraid I might not sink!" said Big Claus.

"It will be all right!" said Little Claus, but he put a stone in the sack all the same, tied the neck fast and gave it a shove. Plop! There was Big Claus, in the river, and down he sank to the bottom. "I'm afraid he won't find the cattle," said Little Claus and, so saying, he drove his cattle home.

# Thumbelina

Once upon a time there was a woman who longed to have a tiny child, but she simply did not know where to find one. So she went to see an old witch and told her: "I long with all my heart to have a little child, won't you tell me where to find one?"

"Oh, we'll soon sort that out!" said the witch. "Here is a grain of barley, not the kind they grow in the farmer's fields, or use to feed the hens, but if you put it in a flower-pot, you'll soon see what happens!"

"Thank you very much," said the woman, giving the witch twelve shilling pieces. Home she went and planted the grain of barley and at once a lovely big flower shot up, which looked just like a tulip, but its petals were tightly closed as if it were still in bud.

"What a wonderful flower," said the woman, kissing the pretty red and yellow petals, but as she kissed them the flower gave a great snap and opened. It really was a tulip, as she could see now, but in the very heart of the flower, on the green stigma, sat a tiny little girl, delicate and graceful, no taller than the length of your thumb, and so she was called Thumbelina.

For a cradle she was given the painted shell of a walnut, with blue violet-petals for her mattress and a rose-petal for her quilt. There she slept at night, but by day she played on the table, on which the woman had placed a dish which she had edged with flowers, their stalks lying in the water. A big tulip leaf floated there, and on that Thumbelina would sit and sail from one side of the dish to the other. She had two white horse's hairs to row with – it was a fine sight! She could sing too, in a voice so rare that no one had heard the like before.

One night, as she was lying in her pretty bed, an ugly toad came hopping in at the window, which had a broken pane. The toad was large, wet and hideous and it hopped right down on the table where Thumbelina lay asleep under the red rose petal.

"She would make a lovely wife for my son," said the toad, and, picking up the walnut shell in which Thumbelina slept, she hopped off with her through the broken pane and into the garden.

The toad lived with her son in the swampy, muddy verge of a broad stream. Her son was as foul and nasty as his mother. "Croak, croak, croak-oak-oak!" was all he could say when he saw the pretty little girl in the walnut shell.

"Don't talk so loud or you'll wake her," said the old toad, "she could easily run away, she's as light as swan's down. We'll put her in the stream on one of the broad water-lily leaves and for her, light and little as she is, it will be like an island. She can't run away from there while we get the house ready under the mud for the two of you to live in."

There were many water-lilies growing in the

stream, all of them with those broad, green leaves which look as though they are floating on the water. The leaf that was furthest out was also the biggest of all and there it was that the old toad left Thumbelina in her walnut shell.

The poor little tiny creature woke up very early next morning and when she saw where she was she began to weep bitterly, for the big green leaf was entirely surrounded by water. There was no way in which she could get back to land.

The old toad sat down in the mud decorating her house with reeds and yellow water flowers – it was to be made really attractive for her new daughter-in-law – and then she swam with her ugly son to the leaf where Thumbelina stood. They had come to fetch her pretty bed which was to be set up in the bridal chamber before she herself arrived. The old toad bowed deep in the water before her, saying: "Here is my son, who is to be your husband, and you will have a beautiful home down in the mud!"

"Croak, croak, croak-oak-oak!" was all the son could say. Then they took the pretty little bed and swam away with it while Thumbelina sat all alone on the green leaf, crying, for she did not want to live with the ugly toad or marry her hideous son. The little fish swimming down there in the water must have seen the toad and heard what she said, because they popped their heads up to have a look at the little girl. As soon as they saw her they thought her so beautiful that it hurt them to think of her living down below with the nasty toad. No, that must never happen! They flocked round the green stalk holding up the leaf on which Thumbelina stood and gnawed it through with their teeth so that the leaf went floating down the stream, carrying Thumbelina away, far away, where the toad could not reach her.

Thumbelina sailed past many strange places and the little birds in the bushes saw her and sang: "What a beautiful maiden she is!" The leaf that bore her floated further and further away, until Thumbelina was carried to foreign countries.

A sweet little white butterfly began to fly round and round her and at last alighted on the leaf, for it had fallen in love with Thumbelina, who was happy now, for the toad could not reach her and it was so delightful sailing along on her leaf. The sun shone on the water like gleaming gold. She took off her sash and tied one end round the butterfly, the other to the leaf, which was travelling much faster now – and so was she, for she was standing on it.

All of a sudden a great maybug flew up, caught sight of her and on the instant it had closed its claws round her slender waist and flown into a tree with her, but the green leaf went floating on down the stream and the butterfly flew with it, because he could not get away.

Lord, but poor little Thumbelina was terrified when the maybug flew into the tree with her! But most of all she was distressed about the pretty white butterfly tied to the leaf, who would now starve to death because he could not get away. But none of that mattered to the maybug, which sat down beside her on the biggest green leaf on the tree, gave her honey from the flowers to eat and told her how beautiful she was, although she was not in the least like a maybug. Then all the other maybugs living in the tree came to visit them. They looked at Thumbelina and the spinster maybugs raised their antennae and said: "But she's only got two legs, how wretched!" "She has no antennae," they said, "her waist is so skinny, ugh! She looks just like a human being, isn't she ugly!" said all the female maybugs, although Thumbelina was so beautiful. The maybug who had picked her up thought so too, but when all the others said she was ugly he began to believe it himself and did not want her any more. She could go where she liked. He flew down from the tree with her and set her down on a daisy, where she cried because she was so ugly that the maybug did not want her, although she was the prettiest creature you could imagine, as delicate and transparent as a rose petal.

Throughout the summer poor Thumbelina

lived all alone in the great wood. She plaited a grass hammock for herself and hung it under a big dock leaf to shield herself from the rain. She ate the honey from the flowers and drank the morning dew from their petals. So summer and autumn passed, but then came winter, the long, cold winter. All the birds who had sung so sweetly for her flew away, trees and flowers withered, the big dock leaf which had been her roof rolled up until it was no more than a faded, yellow stalk, and she was terribly cold, for her clothes were worn out and she herself was so tiny and fragile, poor Thumbelina, that it seemed that she would freeze to death. Soon it began to snow and every snowflake that fell was the same to her as a shovelful would be to us, because we are big and she was no taller than your thumb. So she wrapped herself in a withered leaf, but it was no good, she was still shivering with cold.

Just outside the wood, where she was now, lay a big cornfield, but the corn had gone long ago and only the bare, dry stubble rose out of the frozen earth. The stubble was like a forest to her and as she walked through it she shuddered with cold. Then she came to the fieldmouse's door, a little hole under the stubble. There the fieldmouse kept herself warm and comfortable, with a whole roomful of corn, a nice kitchen and a dining-room. Poor Thumbelina stopped just inside the door like any poor beggar girl and begged for a little piece of one barley corn, because she had had nothing at all to eat for two days.

"You poor little thing!" said the fieldmouse, for she was a good old fieldmouse at heart, "come into my warm house and eat with me!"

Since she had now taken a liking to Thumbelina, she said: "I will gladly have you to stay for the winter, but you must keep my house nice and clean and tell me stories, because that is what I like." And Thumbelina did what the good old fieldmouse asked and led a pleasant life with her.

"We're going to have a visitor soon," the fieldmouse told her, "my neighbour comes to see me once a week. He is even better off than I am, with a big drawing-room and a beautiful velvet coat. If you could get him for a husband you would be well looked after, but he cannot see. You had better tell him the very best stories you know."

But Thumbelina did not do as she said, because the neighbour was a mole and she did not want him at all. He came to visit them in his black velvet coat, very rich and learned, as the fieldmouse said. His home was more than twenty times as big as the fieldmouse's and learned he certainly was, but he could not bear the sun and the pretty flowers and spoke ill of them, because he had never seen them. Thumbelina had to sing for him and she sang both "Fly, maybug, fly!" and "The monk walked in the meadow," and the mole fell in love with her for the sake of her beautiful voice, but he said nothing because he was a sober-minded man.

He had just dug a long corridor for himself from his house to theirs, where the fieldmouse and Thumbelina were allowed to walk as often as they liked. But he asked them not to be afraid of the dead bird which was lying in the corridor. It was a whole bird, with feathers and beak, which must have died just before the winter began and was now buried where he had dug his passage.

The mole picked up a bit of rotten wood in his mouth, for it shines like fire in the darkness, and, walking ahead of them, he lighted their way down the long, dark corridor. When they reached the place where the dead bird lay the mole made a hole in the roof with his broad nose for the light to shine through. In the middle of the passage lay a dead swallow, its pretty wings pressed to its sides, its legs and head drawn in under its feathers. The poor bird must have died of cold. Thumbelina felt so sorry for it, for she loved all the little birds which had sung and twittered so prettily for her all summer long, but the mole gave it a push with his short legs and said: "That won't be cheeping any more – how miserable it must be to be born a bird!

Thank goodness none of my children will be, because a little bird like that has nothing but its twittering and in winter it must die."

"Yes, that's what you would say, being a sensible man," said the fieldmouse, "what good is all its twittering to a bird when winter comes? It is bound to starve and freeze to death – but it must be a good life, too."

Thumbelina said nothing, but when the other two turned their backs on the bird she stooped and kissed its closed eyes. "Perhaps it was the one that sang to me in summertime," she thought. "What joy it gave me then, dear, pretty bird."

The mole stopped the hole up again, blocking out the light, and took the ladies home, but that night Thumbelina could not sleep. She left her bed and wove a big blanket of hay which she carried down and spread over the dead bird, putting soft cotton wool, which she had found in the fieldmouse's room, down its sides so that it should be warm on the cold ground.

"Goodbye, you pretty little bird," she said, "goodbye and thank you for your lovely song in summer when all the trees were green and the sun shone down so warmly on us." She laid her head against the bird's breast – and started back, because there seemed to be something beating inside: the bird's heart. The swallow was not dead but in a swoon and now it was warm it came to life again.

In the autumn all the swallows fly off to the warm countries but any that are delayed freeze and fall down dead, to lie where they fall until the cold snow covers them over.

Thumbelina shook from head to toe, really frightened now, for to her the bird was very, very big, but she plucked up her courage, tucked the cotton wool more tightly round the poor swallow and fetched the curled mint leaf which had been her quilt and laid it over the bird's head.

Next day she crept down to it again and now it was fully conscious, but so weak that it could only open its eyes for a moment to look at Thumbelina standing with a piece of rotten wood in her hand, for she had no other light.

"Thank you, you lovely child," said the sick swallow, "you have warmed me so beautifully that I shall soon regain my strength and be able to fly out in the warm sunshine."

"Oh!" she said, "it is very cold outside, cold and freezing, you stay in your warm bed and I will take care of you."

She brought water to the swallow in a petal and he drank and told her how he had torn a wing on a thorn bush and been unable to fly as fast as the other swallows when they flew away to the warm countries. At last he had fallen to earth, but he could remember no more and had no idea how he had come to this place. The swallow stayed underground all winter, cared for by Thumbelina, who was very fond of him. She told neither the mole nor the fieldmouse what she was doing, because they did not like the poor swallow at all.

As soon as it was spring and the sun began to warm the earth, the swallow said goodbye to Thumbelina, who opened up the hole made by the mole. The sun shone brightly through it and the swallow asked Thumbelina to come with him. Sitting on his back, she could fly with him far out over the green forest. But Thumbelina knew that it would distress the old fieldmouse if she deserted her.

"No, I can't," said Thumbelina.

"Goodbye, goodbye, you good, beautiful girl," said the swallow, and out he flew into the sunshine. Thumbelina watched him, her eyes full of tears, for she was very fond of the poor swallow.

"Tweet, tweet!" sang the bird, flying off into the green forest.

Thumbelina was very unhappy. She was never allowed to go out into the warm sunshine and the corn that the farmer had sown over the fieldmouse's house had grown so high that it was like a dense forest to the poor little girl, who measured only a thumb's length.

"Now you must spend the summer making your trousseau," the fieldmouse told her, for by now their neighbour, the drab mole in his black

velvet coat, had asked her to marry him. "You must have both woollens and linen, cushions and bedding, when you become the mole's wife!"

Thumbelina had to spin by hand and the fieldmouse hired four spiders to spin and weave night and day. Every night the mole came to visit them, and all he talked about was that when the summer was over the sun would not be so hot, for now it baked the earth as hard as a stone. Yes, when the summer was over he would marry Thumbelina, but this gave her no pleasure, for she did not like the drab mole at all. Every morning at sunrise and every evening at dusk she would creep out to the doorway and as the wind parted the ears of corn so that she could see the blue sky she thought how light and beautiful it was out here and longed to see her dear swallow again. But the swallow never came, he must have been flying far away among the beautiful green trees. When autumn came Thumbelina had completed her trousseau.

"You shall be married in a month," the fieldmouse told her, but Thumbelina wept and said she did not want to marry the dull mole.

"Stuff and nonsense!" said the fieldmouse. "Don't you be contrary or I shall bite you with my white teeth. You're getting a fine husband and the queen herself would envy him his black velvet coat. He has both food and drink in plenty, you should thank God for him!"

And so the wedding was arranged. The mole had already arrived to fetch Thumbelina, who was to live with him far below the ground, never to come up into the warm sunshine which the mole hated. The poor child was very wretched at having to bid farewell to the beautiful sun, which she had at least been allowed to see from the doorway when she lived with the fieldmouse.

"Farewell, you bright sun," she said, stretching out her arms, and she took a few steps outside the fieldmouse's house because the corn had been harvested now and only the dry stubble was left. "Farewell, farewell!" she said, flinging her arms round a little red flower.

"Remember me to the little swallow if ever you see him!"

"Tweet, tweet!" came at that moment from above her head. She looked up, and there was the little swallow, who was overjoyed to see Thumbelina. She told him how she was being forced to marry the horrid mole and live deep underground where the sun never shone and she could not help weeping as she spoke.

"The cold winter is coming," said the little swallow, "and I am flying far away to the warm countries, will you come with me? You can sit on my back, only tie yourself on with your sash and we shall fly away from the horrid mole and his dark house, far over the mountains to the warm countries where the sun shines more sweetly than here, where it is always summer, with its beautiful flowers. Fly with me, sweet little Thumbelina, who saved my life when I lay frozen in the dark earth!"

"Yes, I will come with you," said Thumbelina, and climbing on to the bird's back, her feet against its outstretched wings, she tied her sash firmly round the strongest feather. The swallow flew high in the air, over seas and forests, high above the great mountains where the snow always lies, and Thumbelina froze in the cold air, but she crept under the bird's warm feathers, only poking her little head out to see all the beauty below them.

At last they reached the warm countries where the sun shone more brightly than at home, the sky was twice as high and the most beautiful green and blue grapes grew in every hedgerow. Oranges and lemons hung in the orchards, there was a scent of myrtle and mint and lovely children ran down the road playing with big, gaily-coloured butterflies. But the swallow flew on and on and the land grew more and more beautiful. Under the green trees beside a blue lake stood a shining white marble palace from ancient days, with vines twining themselves round the tall pillars. At the top of them there were many swallows' nests and in one of these Thumbelina's swallow lived.

"This is my house," said the swallow, "but

if you would like to choose one of the glorious flowers growing down there for yourself, I will set you down on it and you shall have all the happiness you desire."

"That would be lovely," she said, clapping her little hands.

One of the great marble pillars had collapsed on the ground and broken in three, but between the fragments grew the prettiest white flowers. The swallow flew down with Thumbelina and set her on one of the broad petals, but what was her astonishment when in the middle of the flower she saw a tiny man, as white and transparent as if he were made of glass. He was wearing a beautiful golden crown on his head and had delicate white wings on his shoulders, although he was no bigger than Thumbelina herself. He was the angel of the flower and in each flower there lived a tiny man or woman, but this was the king of them all.

"Oh God, how handsome he is!" Thumbelina whispered to the swallow. The little prince was afraid of the swallow, which was a giant to him, tiny and slender as he was, but when he saw Thumbelina he was overjoyed. She was the very prettiest girl he had ever seen and at once he took the golden crown off his own head and put it on hers, asked her name and if she would marry him and become queen of all the flowers. Oh yes, this was indeed a man, nothing like the toad's son or the mole in the black velvet coat. So Thumbelina accepted the handsome prince and from each flower there stepped a little lady or gentleman, each one a delight to the eye. Each had a present for Thumbelina, but the best present of all was a pair of wings from a big white fly. When they were attached to Thumbelina's back she too could fly from flower to flower. There was great rejoicing and the little swallow sat in his nest singing his best songs for them, although his heart was sore because he loved Thumbelina dearly and never wanted to be parted from her.

"You shall not be called Thumbelina," the flower angel told her, "it is an ugly name and you are so beautiful. We will call you Maya."

"Farewell, farewell!" called the little swallow when it flew away from the warm countries again to far off Denmark. There it had a little nest over the window of the man who tells fairy tales. "Tweet, tweet!" sang the swallow, and that is how we know the story.

# The Tinderbox

A soldier came marching down the road. One, two! One, two! He had his knapsack on his back and a sword at his side, for he had been in the war and now he was going home. On the road he met an ugly old witch whose lower lip hung right down to her chest.

"Good evening, soldier," she said. "What a fine sword you have, and what a big knapsack, you're a proper soldier, you are. You shall have as much money as you want!"

"Thank you very much, old witch," said the soldier.

"Do you see that big tree?" asked the witch, pointing to the tree beside them. "It's completely hollow inside. You climb up there and you'll see a hole you can slip through which will take you right inside the tree. I shall tie a rope round you so that I can hoist you up again when you shout."

"And what am I supposed to do in the tree?" asked the soldier.

"Fetch the money!" said the witch. "Let me tell you, when you reach the bottom of the tree you will find yourself in a big passageway. It's quite light, because more than a hundred lamps are burning down there. You will see three doors, which you can open, the key is in the lock. Go into the first room and in the middle of the floor you will see a big chest with a dog sitting on top. It has a pair of eyes as big as teacups, but never you mind about that! I'll give you my blue checked apron to spread out on the floor. You go in quickly, pick up the dog, put him down on my apron, unlock the chest and take out as much money as you like. Those

are all copper coins, but if you'd rather have silver, go to the next room. There's a dog in there with eyes as big as mill wheels, but don't you bother about that, put it on my apron and take the money! On the other hand, if you want gold, you can have that too, as much as you can carry, if you go into the third room. But the dog that sits on the money chest in there has eyes as big as towers. That's a proper dog, I can tell you; but don't you bother about that. Put it on my apron and it won't harm you and you can take as much gold as you want from the chest!"

"That sounds all right," said the soldier, "but what shall I give you, old witch? I should think you'd want something for yourself."

"No," said the witch, "I don't want a single shilling. Just pick up an old tinderbox for me that my grandmother forgot when she was last down there!"

"Well, tie the rope round me," said the soldier.

"There it is," said the witch, "and here is my blue checked apron."

The soldier climbed up the tree, let himself drop into the hollow and just as the witch had said, he found himself standing in a wide passageway where hundreds of lamps were burning.

He opened the first door. Ooh! The dog with eyes as big as teacups sat glaring at him.

"You're a fine fellow," said the soldier, and putting the dog on the witch's apron, he took as many copper coins as his pockets would hold, closed the chest, put the dog back on top of it and went to the next room. Eeyah! There was

the dog with eyes as big as a pair of mill wheels.

"You don't need to look at me like that," said the soldier, "you'll get eye-ache!" And he put the dog down on the witch's apron, but as soon as he saw all the silver coins in the chest he emptied his pockets of the copper coins he had taken and refilled both them and his knapsack with silver. Then he entered the third room – oh, how dreadful! The dog in there really had eyes as big as round towers and they spun in its head like wheels.

"Good evening!" said the soldier, touching his cap, for he had never seen anything like this dog before. But after he had looked at it for a little while he thought, "That's enough," lifted it onto the floor and unlocked the chest. Lord bless us and save us, what a lot of gold there was! He could buy the whole of Copenhagen for it, and the baker's sugar pig, and all the toy soldiers, whips and rocking-horses in the world. Oh yes, that really was money.

The soldier threw out all the silver coins with which he had filled his pockets and knapsack and filled them with gold instead; in fact he filled all his pockets, his knapsack, his cap and his boots so full that he could barely walk. He was rich now.

He put the dog back on the chest, slammed the door and shouted from the hollow tree:

"Hoist me up now, old witch!"

"Have you got the tinderbox?" asked the witch.

"That's true," said the soldier, "I'd forgotten all about it." Back he went and picked it up, the witch hoisted him out of the tree and there he was, back on the road with pockets, boots, knapsack and cap filled with money.

"What do you want the tinderbox for?" the soldier asked.

"That's none of your business," said the witch, "you've got the money, give me the tinderbox!"

"Hoity-toity!" said the soldier, "tell me at once what you want it for or I'll draw my sword and cut off your head."

"No!" said the witch.

So the soldier cut off her head. There she lay, but the soldier poured all his money into her apron, and, with the bundle on his back and the tinderbox in his pocket, he walked into town.

It was a nice town and the soldier walked into the nicest inn and demanded the best rooms and his favourite food, because he was rich now, with all that money.

The servant who was cleaning his boots thought they were an odd pair of old boots for such a rich gentleman, but that was before he bought himself new ones. The next day he had boots fit to walk in and a handsome suit of clothes. The soldier had become a fine gentleman now and the people told him about all the good things in their town and about their king and his beautiful daughter, the princess.

"How can I get to see her?" asked the soldier.

"No one can get to see her at all," said all the people, "she lives in a great copper castle surrounded by walls and towers. No one but the king dares visit her, because it has been foretold that she will marry a common soldier and that's not to the king's liking."

"I should certainly like to see her," thought the soldier, but there was absolutely no chance of that.

He was living a pleasant life now, going to the theatre, driving through the king's park and giving money to the poor, which was nice of him. He well remembered what it was like not to have a penny to his name. He was rich now, he wore elegant clothes and had many friends who said he was a rare one, a real cavalier, and the soldier enjoyed that. But since he handed money out every day and never got any back again, in the end he was left with barely two shillings to his name and he had to move out of the fine room he had been living in and up into a little garret room right under the roof, where he polished his own boots and mended his socks with a darning needle and none of his friends came to see him because there were too many stairs to climb.

One dark evening when he could not even

buy himself a candle he remembered that there was a candle-end in the tinderbox he had picked up in the hollow tree where the witch had sent him. He took out the tinderbox and the candle-end, but as soon as he struck the flint and the sparks flew, the door sprang open and the dog with eyes as big as teacups stood before him.

"What is my master's command?" it said.

"What's all this?" said the soldier, "that's a funny kind of tinderbox, will it really give me anything I want? Get me some money!" he told the dog, and hey presto it had gone, and hey presto it was back again, with a bagful of coins in its mouth.

Now the soldier knew what a wonderful tinderbox it was. If he struck it once, the dog that sat on the chest full of copper came, if he struck it twice, the one that sat on the silver chest came and, if he struck it three times, the one with the gold came. The soldier moved down again to his handsome rooms, got himself some good clothes and suddenly all his friends knew him and were very fond of him again.

One day he thought to himself: "It really is very odd that one can't even see the princess. Everyone says she's very beautiful, but what's the good of that if she's always shut up in that big copper castle with all those towers? Is it really impossible for me to see her? Where is my tinderbox?" And he struck the flint and hey presto the dog with eyes as big as teacups stood before him.

"I know it's the middle of the night," said the soldier, "but I am simply longing to see the princess, if only for a moment."

The dog left at once and before the soldier could even think, it was back again with the princess, lying asleep on the dog's back. She was so beautiful that anyone could see she was a real princess. The soldier could not help himself, he had to kiss her, for he was a proper soldier.

The dog took the princess straight home, but when it was morning and the king and queen were taking tea with her, the princess said she had dreamed a wonderful dream the night before, about a dog and a soldier. She had ridden on the dog and the soldier had kissed her.

"That's a pretty story," said the queen.

One of the old ladies-in-waiting was told to watch by the princess's bed the next night to see if it had been a real dream or something else.

The soldier longed passionately to see the beautiful princess again and so the dog came back that night, picked her up and ran as fast as it could, but the old lady-in-waiting put on her waterproof boots and ran swiftly behind it. When she saw it disappearing inside a big house she thought: "Now I know the place," and with a piece of chalk she drew a big cross on the door. Then she went home to bed, but when the dog took the princess home again he saw the cross on the door of the soldier's house and he too took a piece of chalk and drew crosses on all the doors in town. That was cunning of him, for now the lady-in-waiting could not find the right door, since there were crosses everywhere. Early in the morning the king and queen, the old lady-in-waiting and all the court officials went to see where the princess had been.

"There it is!" said the king, when he saw the first door with a cross on it.

"No, it's there, my sweet husband!" said the queen, seeing a second door with a cross on it.

"But there's one there, and one there," they all said, seeing the crosses on all the doors. Then they realized that it was no use looking any longer.

But the queen was a very intelligent woman, who could do more than sit in a royal carriage. With her big golden scissors she cut out a big piece of silk and made it into a pretty little bag which she filled with buckwheat groats. She tied the bag on the princess's back and then she snipped a little hole in the bag so that the groats would trickle out along the way the princess went.

That night the dog came again, put the princess on its back and ran with her to the soldier who loved her so much and longed to be a prince so that he could marry her.

The dog did not notice the groats trickling behind it from the castle to the soldier's window, where it climbed up the wall with the princess, so in the morning the king and queen could see quite clearly where their daughter had been and the soldier was arrested and put in gaol.

There he sat, in the dreary darkness and they told him: "You're to be hanged tomorrow!" That was not an amusing thing to hear and he had left his tinderbox at home in the inn. In the morning he watched through the iron bars in the little window as people hurried from the town to see him hanged. He heard the drums and saw the soldiers marching, and everyone came running. There was a cobbler's boy too, in his leather apron and slippers, running so

hard that one of his slippers flew off and hit the wall where the soldier was looking out between the iron bars.

"Hi, cobbler's boy, don't be in such a hurry!" said the soldier. "There will be nothing doing until I get there; but if you will run to the place where I lived and get me my tinderbox, you shall have four shillings, but you'd better be quick about it!"

The cobbler's boy was very keen to have the four shillings and sped away to get the tinderbox. He brought it to the soldier and – this is what happened next.

Outside the town a tall gallows had been erected, and the soldiers and hundreds of thousands of people were now standing round

it. The king and queen sat on their grand throne facing the judge and the supreme council.

The soldier was already standing on the platform, but as they were about to put the rope round his neck he reminded them that before paying the penalty a sinner was always granted one innocent wish. All he wanted was a pipeful of tobacco, the last pipe he would ever smoke in this world.

The king would not deny him that and the soldier took out his tinderbox and struck it, once, twice, thrice! All three dogs appeared, the one with eyes as big as teacups, the one with eyes like mill wheels and the one with eyes as big as round towers.

"Now get me out of being hanged!" said the soldier, and the dogs rushed at the judges and the council, grabbing one by the legs and another by the nose and flung them so high in the air that when they fell back again they broke in pieces.

"Leave me alone!" said the king, but the biggest dog took him and the queen together and threw them after all the others. The soldiers were terrified and the people shouted: "Little soldier, you shall be our king and marry the beautiful princess!"

So the soldier sat in the king's carriage and all three dogs danced ahead of it shouting "Hurrah" and the boys whistled through their fingers and the soldiers presented arms. The princess came out of the copper castle and became queen, which she enjoyed very much. The marriage feast lasted a week and the dogs sat at the table with them and feasted their eyes.

# The Princess and the Pea

Once upon a time there was a prince who wanted to marry a princess, but she had to be a *real* princess. He travelled the world to find one but wherever he went there was something wrong. There were princesses in plenty, but he was never quite sure if they were *real* princesses, there was always something that was not quite right.

At last he came home again, very miserable, for he longed to marry a real princess.

One evening a terrible storm broke, with lightning and thunder and pouring rain, quite dreadful. There came a knocking at the town gate and the old king went down to open it.

A princess stood outside, but God knows what she looked like, in all that rain and foul weather. The water was streaming down her hair and clothes, running in at the toes of her shoes and out at the heels, and yet she said she was a real princess.

"Well, we shall soon find out!" thought the old queen, but she said nothing. Going to the bedroom she took all the bedclothes off and placed one pea on the bedstead. On it she put twenty mattresses and another twenty eiderdown quilts on top of the mattresses.

That was where the princess was to sleep that night.

In the morning they asked her how she had slept.

"Oh, terribly badly!" said the princess, "I scarcely closed my eyes all night. God knows what was in the bed, but I was lying on something so hard that I am black and blue all over. It was terrible."

Then they knew that this was a real princess, since she had felt the pea through twenty mattresses and twenty eiderdown quilts. Only a real princess could be so sensitive.

The princess took her to wife, since he knew that he would be marrying a real princess, and the pea went into the art collection and, unless someone has stolen it, it is there still.

There, that was a real story!

# The Snowman

"I'm creaking fit to burst with cold!" said the snowman. "The wind really bites some life into you, and how that flaming thing up there glares!" He meant the sun, which was just about to set. "It's not going to make me blink, I'll keep my fragments fixed." These were the two big triangular fragments of tile which were the snowman's eyes; his mouth was a piece of an old rake, so he had teeth.

He had been born to the cheers of the boys, greeted by the sound of bells and the crack of whips from the sledges.

The sun went down, the full moon came up, huge and round, bright and beautiful in the blue sky.

"There she is, coming back from the other side," said the snowman, who thought it was the sun reappearing. "I've stopped her glaring now and she can just hang there shining so that I can see myself. If only I knew how to move! I would love to move, and if I could I would go and slide on the ice like the boys, but I don't know how to run."

72

"Gone, gone!" barked the old watchdog; he was rather hoarse nowadays because he had once been a housedog and slept under the stove. "The sun will teach you how to run! I saw it happen to the one before you and the one before that, gone, gone! All gone."

"I don't understand you, friend," said the snowman. "Do you mean that thing up there will teach me how to run?" He meant the moon. "Yes, she ran right enough when I gave her a hard stare and now she's crept up on me from a different quarter."

"You don't know anything," said the watchdog, "but of course you've only just been slapped together! The one you can see now is called the moon and the one that's gone was the sun. The sun will be back tomorrow morning and it will be able to teach you to run down to the ditch. There's going to be a change in the weather soon, I know, because I've got shooting pains in my left hind leg."

"I don't understand him," said the snowman, "but I have a feeling he's being nasty. And that one that glared and went down, the one he calls the sun, I have a feeling that's not my friend either."

"Gone, gone!" barked the watchdog and, walking round itself three times, it lay down to sleep in its kennel.

Sure enough, the weather changed. In the early morning a thick, damp fog lay over the fields, lifting at daybreak. The wind was so icy that the frost set hard, but what a sight it was when the sun rose! All the trees and bushes were thick with rime like a forest of white corals, all the trees seemed to be hung with brilliant white flowers. Now the countless delicate twigs, which are covered up by the leaves in summertime, stood out singly, making a pattern of lace so white that a bright light shone from every branch. The weeping birches moved in the wind, as lively as the trees in summertime. When the sun shone down on all this matchless beauty it sparkled as if powdered with diamond dust and, over the snowy blanket on the ground, shone bigger diamonds, or else they resembled countless tiny candles, still whiter than the whitest snow.

"Did you ever see anything so beautiful?" said a girl who had just stepped out into the garden with a young man and stopped by the snowman to look at the glittering trees. "It's no more beautiful than this in summer," she said, her eyes shining.

"And you don't get a chap like that in summertime either," said the young man, pointing to the snowman. "He's wonderful."

The girl laughed, nodded to the snowman and danced away with her friend, across the snow which squeaked beneath their feet as if they were walking on starch.

"Who were those two?" the snowman asked the watchdog. "You've been on the farm longer than I have, do you know them?"

"Indeed I do!" said the watchdog. "She has patted me and he has given me a marrow bone; I shan't bite them."

"But why are they behaving like that?" asked the snowman.

"They're going to be marrrrr-ried!" said the watchdog. "They're going to move to another kennel and gnaw the same bone. Gone! Gone!"

"Are those two as important as you and I?" asked the snowman.

"They are our masters," said the watchdog. "People who were born yesterday really do know extraordinarily little, I see! I'm old and wise; I know everyone on the farm and I remember a time when I didn't stand out here in the cold on guard: gone! Gone!"

"I love the cold," said the snowman. "Go on talking! But you mustn't rattle your chain, it makes me feel weak inside."

"Gone, gone," barked the watchdog. "I was a puppy once, a little darling, so they said, and I used to lie on a velvet chair inside the house; I could lie on the master's lap and they would kiss my face and wipe my paws with embroidered handkerchiefs. They called me 'Sweetest' and 'Puddypaws', but then I got too big for them and they gave me to the housekeeper. I had to live in the cellar then; you can

see straight into it from where you are, down into the room where I was master – that's how it was with the housekeeper. Of course it wasn't as grand as upstairs, but it was more comfortable: there were no children to hug me and pull me about and my food was just as good and there was more of it! I had my own pillow and there was a stove, which is the most wonderful thing in the world in this season. I used to crawl right underneath it and disappear. Oh, I still dream of that stove: gone! Gone!"

"Are stoves as beautiful as all that?" asked the snowman. "Are they like me?"

"They are exactly the opposite of you. This stove is coal-black and it has a long neck with a brass collar round it. It eats firewood and blows out flames. You have to keep to one side, close in, right underneath; there's nothing more comfortable in the world. You must be able to see it through that window from where you're standing."

The snowman looked and sure enough he saw a black polished object with a brass cylinder and a fire blazing out at the bottom. The snowman felt very strange, he had a feeling that he himself could not understand, something he had never known before but which all human beings know, unless they are snowmen.

"And why did you leave her?" he asked, for he felt that the housekeeper must have been a she. "How could you leave a place like that?"

"I was made to go," said the watchdog. "They threw me out and chained me up here. I had bitten the youngest child in the leg because he had pulled my bone away: a bone for a bone, I thought! But they were very angry and, from that time on, I've been chained up here and lost my voice, can't you hear how hoarse I am? Gone! Gone! That was the end of it."

The snowman stopped listening after that. He went on gazing down into the housekeeper's basement room where the stove stood on its four legs, just the same size as the snowman himself.

"There's such a strange creaking inside me," he said. "Can I never get into that room? It's an innocent wish and our innocent wishes must surely be fulfilled. It's my greatest wish, my only wish, and it would be quite unfair if it could not be satisfied. I must get in, I must lean against her, even if I have to break the window."

"You'll never get in there," said the watchdog, "and once you got to the stove you'd be gone! Gone!"

"I'm as good as gone now," said the snowman, "I think I'm coming apart."

All day long the snowman stood looking in at the window; at dusk the room became even more inviting, with the soft glow from the stove which was lit by neither sun nor moon but by the light that only a stove can give when there is something in it. When someone opened the door the flames would shoot out – that was their way; then the snowman's white face blushed red and the red light was reflected all over his chest.

"I can't bear it," he said, "how becoming it is when she puts her tongue out like that!"

The night was very long but not too long for the snowman, sunk in his own delightful thoughts, which froze until he creaked.

When day dawned the basement windows were covered with the most beautiful frost flowers any snowman could have wished, had they not hidden the stove from him. The panes would not thaw, he could not see her. The frosty snow creaked and crackled fit to delight a snowman, but he was not delighted; he could and should have been happy, but he was not happy, he was stove-sick.

"That's a bad illness for a snowman," said the watchdog, "I used to suffer from that sickness too, but I've got over it: gone! gone! – and now the weather's going to change."

The weather changed, the thaw began.

The thaw increased, the snowman shrank. He said not a word, he never complained and that is a sure sign.

One morning he collapsed. There was something like a broom handle left standing where

he had stood, the centre round which the boys
had built him.

"Now I can understand that sickness of his!"
said the watchdog. "The snowman had a poker
down his middle and that was what was moving
inside him and now its over: gone! gone!"

And soon the winter was over too.

"Gone, gone!" barked the watchdog, but on
the farm the little girls sang:

"The scented woodruff's flowers are out,
The silken willow catkins sprout.
The cuckoos chime, the skylarks sing:
In February comes the spring.
I sing with them, Cuckoo! Tweet, tweet!
Come, lovely sun, give us your heat!"

And nobody remembered the snowman.

# The Ugly Duckling

It was summertime and the countryside was beautiful: the corn stood golden in the fields, the wheat was green, hay had been stacked down in the green meadow and the stork was walking up and down on his long, red legs talking Egyptian, the language he had learned from his mother. The fields and meadows were surrounded by forests and in the midst of the forests lay deep pools. Oh yes, the countryside was certainly beautiful. In all this sunshine there lay an ancient castle surrounded by a deep moat and from the base of its walls to the water's edge grew dock weeds so tall that little children could stand upright under them. It was as wild in there as a dense wood and a duck had chosen this place for her nest. She was waiting to hatch her ducklings but she was becoming sick and tired of sitting; it had taken so long now and scarcely anyone came to visit her. The other ducks preferred swimming in the moat to sitting under the dock leaves for a chat.

At last one egg after another began to crack. "Peep, peep!" they said: all the egg-yolks had suddenly come to life and were poking their heads out.

"Quack, quack, quick, quick!" said the mother duck, and out they hurried, as fast as they could, looking all about them under the green leaves, which the mother duck encouraged because green is good for the eyes.

"What a big world it is!" said all the baby ducks, because they had a great deal more room now than when they were curled up inside their eggs.

"Do you think this is the whole world?" said their mother. "It stretches a long way past the other side of the wheat fields, right down to the priest's land, though I have never been there myself. Are you all here now?" She rose to her feet. "No, here's the biggest egg, how long is that going to take? I'm so tired of sitting!" And down she sat again.

"Well, how's it going?" asked an old duck who had come to see her.

"This big egg is taking such a long time," said the sitting duck, "it simply won't hatch! But you must look at the others, they're the prettiest ducklings I've ever seen. All of them are just like their father, that rascal who has never come to see me."

"Let me see that egg that won't hatch," said the old duck. "You mark my words, it's a turkey's egg. I was fooled that way once too, and I had plenty of trouble with those turkey chicks, because they're afraid of the water, I can tell you. I could not get them in, I quacked and snapped, but it was no use. Let me see that egg. Yes, it's a turkey's egg! You leave it there and teach the other children to swim!"

"I'll just sit on it a little longer," said the mother duck. "I've been here such a long time now I may as well wait until the deer park is mown."

"Just as you like," said the old duck, marching off.

At last the big egg cracked. "Peep, peep!" said the baby, tumbling out; what a big ugly thing he was! The duck looked at him. "That is a terribly big duckling," she said, "none of the others look like that, but surely it can't be a turkey chick? Well, we'll soon see: into the water with him, if I have to kick him there myself."

The next day the weather was simply beautiful. The sun shone down on all the green dock leaves and the mother duck with all her family went down to the moat. Splash! She jumped into the water.

"Quack, quack!" she said, and in plopped one duckling after another. The water came up over their heads but they popped straight up again and floated beautifully, their legs working all by themselves. They were all in the water, even the ugly grey baby. "No, that's no turkey," she said, "look how beautifully he uses his legs, how straight he holds himself, that's my own child. He's quite handsome really, if you take a good look at him, quack, quack! Come along with me now and I'll take you out into the wide world and introduce you to the other ducks, but keep close to me all the time so that no one steps on you, and watch out for the cat!"

In the farm yard there was a tremendous row going on because two families were squabbling over an eel's head, which the cat got in the end.

"There, that's what the world is like!" said the mother duck, licking her beak, for she too would have liked the eel's head. "Use your legs," she said, "show that you can quack nicely and duck your head to the old duck over there. She's the noblest of them all and she has Spanish blood, so she's fat and as you see she's got a red rag tied round her leg, which is extremely beautiful and the greatest distinction a duck can receive. It means that they won't do away with her and that she will be recognized by man and beast. Quack, quack, no knock-knees now, a well brought-up duck walks with its legs far apart like its father and mother. There now, bow your necks and say: Quack!"

And they did, but the other ducks looked at them and made loud remarks: "Oh look, now we've got to put up with that brood as well, as if there weren't enough of us already, and, phew, look at that duckling there, we're not having that!" And one duck flew at the ugly duckling and bit it in the neck.

"Let him alone!" said his mother, "he's not done you any harm."

"Yes, but he's too big and different," said the duck which had bitten him, "and that's why he needs roughing up."

"Those are fine ducklings," said the old duck with the rag round her leg, "all fine ducklings, except for that one, which is not a success and I would rather you tried again!"

"That can't be done, Your Grace," said the mother duck. "He's not handsome, but he's very good-natured and swims as nicely as any of the others; in fact, I believe he swims better. I think he'll be better looking as he grows up, or perhaps he'll get a bit smaller, because he was in the egg too long and that's why he's the wrong shape." She straightened his neck feathers and smoothed him down.

"In any case, he's a drake," she said, "so it doesn't matter too much. I think he's going to be strong, he'll get by!"

"The other ducklings are charming," said the old duck. "Make yourself at home now, and if you should find an eel's head, you may bring it to me."

They made themselves at home, but the poor duckling which had been the last to hatch out and looked so ugly was nipped, shoved and jeered at by both ducks and chickens. "He's too big," they all said, and the turkey cock, who had been born with spurs and thought himself an emperor, puffed himself up like a ship in full sail, made straight for the duckling and attacked him, gobbling and turning red in the

face. The poor duckling did not know whether to stay or run away. He was most unhappy because he looked so ugly and was mocked by all the ducks in the yard.

So the first day passed and after that things got worse and worse. The poor duckling was chased about by everyone, even his brothers and sisters were mean to him, quacking: "I hope the cat takes you, you ugly creature!" And the mother duck said: "If only you were far away!" The ducks bit him and the girl who was supposed to feed them kicked him.

So the duckling flew off over the hedge and the little birds in the bushes started up in terror.

"That's because I'm so ugly," thought the duckling, closing his eyes but he went on running away until he reached the great marsh where the wild ducks lived. There he stayed all night, weary and sorrowful.

In the morning the wild ducks flew up to take a look at their new companion. "What sort of bird are you?" they asked, and the duckling turned from one side to the other, greeting them as politely as he could.

"You're awfully ugly," said the wild ducks, "but that doesn't bother us, as long as you don't marry into our family." The poor duckling had not been considering marriage; if only he could be allowed to stay among the reeds and drink a little marsh water.

There he lay for two whole days, until two wild geese arrived, or rather two wild ganders. They had not long left the egg and therefore went straight to the point.

"Look, chum," they said, "you're so ugly that we like you. Would you like to come with us and be a migrant? In another marsh nearby there are some sweet and lovely wild geese, all unmarried, and you might make your fortune, ugly as you are."

*Bang! Bang!* Shots rang out at that very moment, and the two wild ganders fell dead among the rushes, staining the water with their blood. *Bang! Bang!* – more shots, and whole flocks of wild geese flew up from the rushes and the guns fired again. The hunt was on. The huntsmen were lying all round the marsh; some of them had even climbed into the trees whose branches hung over the reeds. The blue smoke rose like clouds among the dark trees and hung low over the water. Into the mud waded the gun dogs, splash, splash! Reeds and rushes swayed on all sides, terrifying the poor duckling, who turned his head to tuck it under his wing, but at that very moment he saw a dreadfully big dog almost on top of him, its tongue hanging out of its mouth and its eyes gleaming cruelly. It put its muzzle close to the duckling, baring its sharp teeth – and splash, it turned away without touching the little bird.

"Oh, thank God!" sighed the duckling, "I'm so ugly that even the dog did not want to bite me."

And it lay quite still while a hail of bullets fell among the reeds and shot after shot rang out.

Silence fell late in the day, but the poor duckling still did not dare to show himself. He waited several hours before putting his head up and taking a look round. Then he hurried away from the swamp as fast as he could go, running across fields and meadows, bracing himself with difficulty against the strong wind that had come up.

Towards evening he reached a poor little peasant's hut, so wretched that it could not make up its mind which way to fall and therefore remained standing. The wind was roaring round the duckling, who had to sit on his tail to resist it. As it blew harder and harder he noticed that the door was hanging loose on one hinge, leaving just enough room for him to steal through the gap.

In the hut lived an old woman with her cat and her hen. The cat, which she called Sonny, could arch its back and purr, it could even give off sparks, but only if you rubbed its fur up the wrong way. The hen had very thin, short legs, so it was called Clucky Shortlegs. It laid good eggs and the woman loved it as if it were her own child.

In the morning the strange duckling was noticed at once and the cat began to purr and the hen to cluck.

"What's this?" said the woman, looking round, but her sight was not good, so she thought the ugly duckling was a fat duck which had lost its way. "That is a fine catch," she said, "now I can eat ducks' eggs, as long as it's not a drake. We'll have to see."

So the duckling was taken in on three weeks' trial, but there were no eggs. Now, the cat was master of the house and the hen its mistress and they kept on talking of "we and the world," for they thought they made up half the world, and the best half at that. The duckling thought there might be another opinion, but the hen was not having that.

"Can you lay eggs?" she asked.

"No."

"All right, then hold your tongue!"

And the cat said: "Can you arch your back, purr and give off sparks?"

"No."

"In that case you're not entitled to an opinion when sensible folk are talking!"

So the duckling sat in the corner in a bad

mood, until he remembered the fresh air and the sunshine. Then he was overcome by such a strong desire to float on the water that at last he could not bear it, he had to tell the hen.

"What are you thinking of?" she asked. "You've got nothing to do, that's why you get these fancies. Lay eggs or purr, they'll soon pass!"

"But it's wonderful floating on the water," said the duckling, "wonderful to feel it wash over your head as you dive to the bottom."

"Oh yes, that must be a great pleasure," said the hen, "I think you must have gone mad! Ask the cat, he's the brightest fellow I know, if he likes floating on the water or diving! Never mind what *I* think.

"Ask our mistress herself, the old woman, there's no one in the world wiser than she is. Do you think she wants to go floating about and get her head under water?"

"You don't understand me," said the duckling.

"Oh, so we don't understand you, and who else would? You surely don't think that you're cleverer than the cat and the mistress, not to speak of me! Don't put on airs, child! And thank your maker for all the kindness you have received! Haven't you got a warm room and company you can learn something from? But you're such a stupid, it's no fun talking to you. Believe me, I'm thinking of your own good, I tell you disagreeable things and that's how you can recognize your real friends. Just get on and lay some eggs and learn to purr or give off sparks!"

"I think I shall go out into the wide world," said the duckling.

"Yes, do that!" said the hen.

So the duckling went. He floated on the water, he dived to the bottom, but he was so ugly that all the other creatures ignored him.

Now autumn had come, the leaves in the wood turned yellow and brown and danced in the wind and the air looked cold. The clouds were heavy with hail and snow and the raven on the fence screamed "Ow, ow!" with sheer cold. Yes, it makes you shiver even to think of it, so the poor duckling was certainly having a bad time.

One evening, against a splendid sunset, a whole flock of beautiful great birds flew out of the bushes. The duckling had never seen anything so lovely as their shining, white feathers and long, graceful necks. They were swans, giving their strange cry as they spread their magnificent wings and flew away from the cold regions to warmer lands and lakes that would not freeze over. They rose higher and higher and the ugly little duckling was overcome by a strange feeling. He spun round in the water like a wheel, stretching his neck as far as he could, and gave a cry so high and strange that he even frightened himself. Oh, he could never forget those beautiful birds, those happy birds! When he could no longer see them he dived right to the bottom and when he rose again he was quite beside himself. He did not know what those birds were called or where they were flying, but he loved them as he had loved nothing in his life before. He did not even envy them, it would not have entered his mind to wish for such beauty, he would have been glad if only the ducks could have put up with him – poor, ugly creature.

That winter was very, very cold. The duckling had to swim round and round in the water to prevent it from freezing over, but every night the hole he swam in grew smaller and smaller. The freezing ice-crust creaked. The duckling had to keep on paddling to prevent the water from closing over but at last he was so exhausted that he stopped and was frozen into the ice.

Early next morning a farmer saw him, went out and broke the ice with his clog and carried the duckling home to his wife, who revived him.

The children tried to play with him, but the duckling thought they were going to hurt him and in his fear he flew straight into the milk-pail, splashing the milk all over the room. The farmer's wife screamed and beat the air with her hands and the duckling flew into the butter trough and then into the flour-barrel and out

again; he did look a sight! The farmer's wife screamed and hit out at him with the poker and the children tumbled over each other trying to catch him, laughing and screaming. It was a good thing the door had been left open: out shot the duckling among the bushes in the newly-fallen snow and lay there, almost unconscious.

But it would be far too depressing to recount all the misery and want the duckling had to suffer in that hard winter. He was lying in the marsh among the reeds when the sun began to shine warmly again, larks sang and it was spring.

Then he stretched wings which lifted more strongly than before and carried him power-fully into the air. Before he knew it he was in a big garden where the apple trees were in bloom and the fragrant lilac flowers hung from their long green branches over a winding waterway. It was beautiful there, in all the freshness of

spring, and just ahead of him three beautiful white swans came out of the shelter of the trees, ruffling up their feathers and floating lightly across the water. The duckling recognized the splendid creatures and was overcome by a strange melancholy.

"I shall fly to those royal birds and if they want to cut me to bits because I dare to approach them, ugly as I am, no matter, better to be killed by them than nipped by the ducks, scratched by the hens, kicked by the girl who feeds them and suffer the winter's cold." And he flew down to the water and swam towards the splendid swans. They saw him, ruffled their feathers and began to swim towards him. "Kill me!" said the poor creature, bowing his head towards the surface of the water and awaiting death – but what did he see? Beneath him he saw his own reflection, but he was no longer a clumsy, dirty grey bird, ugly and unsightly. He was a swan himself. It doesn't matter if you are born in a duck's nest as long as you come from a swan's egg.

He was glad to have suffered so much hardship and misery, for it made him appreciate his good fortune and the beauty that had come to him now. The big swans swam round him, stroking him with their beaks.

Some children came into the garden with bread and corn for the swans. The smallest child shouted: "There's a new one!" and the others joined in, "Yes, a new one has arrived!" and clapped their hands and danced about. They ran for their father and mother, bread and cake were tossed on the water and they all said: "The new one is the handsomest – so young and beautiful!" The old swans bowed to him.

The young swan felt so shy that he tucked his head between his wings in confusion. He was overjoyed, but not at all proud, because a good heart is never proud. He remembered how he had been persecuted and derided, and now everyone was saying he was the most beautiful of all beautiful birds. The lilacs bowed their branches to him, right down to the water, and the sun shone warm and kindly. Then he preened his feathers, lifted his slender neck and his heart rejoiced: "I never dreamed of so much happiness when I was the ugly duckling!"

# Booby Jack

In an old manor house out in the country lived an old squire who had two sons who were so witty that half of them would have been enough. They wanted to marry the king's daughter and they felt brave enough to ask, for she had made a proclamation that she would marry the man who could speak up for himself best.

The two sons made their preparations for a week, which was all the time they had, but it was long enough, because they had had a good grounding and that's useful. One of them knew the whole Latin dictionary by heart and also the town newspaper for the last three years, both forwards and backwards. The other had familiarized himself with all the guild articles and what every guild-master should know, so that he could discuss politics, or so he thought, and he could embroider braces, too, with his fine, nimble fingers.

"I shall get the king's daughter," they said, and their father gave them each a fine horse, a coal-black one to the son who knew the dictionary and newspapers by heart and a milk-white one to the son who was as clever as a guild-master and could do embroidery. Then they greased the corners of their mouths with cod-liver oil to help them talk easily. All the servants were waiting outside to see them mount, when out came the third brother, for there were three of them, but no one counted him as a brother, because he was not as learned as the other two and they called him Booby Jack.

"Where are you going in all your Sunday best?" he asked.

"To court, to win the king's daughter with our cleverness. Haven't you heard what the drums have been saying all over the country?" And they told him the news.

"Bless me, then I must go too!" said Booby Jack, but his brothers laughed at him and rode away.

"Father, let me have a horse!" cried Booby Jack. "I've just got a mind to marry. If she takes me, she takes me, and if she doesn't, I'll take her all the same."

"What nonsense," said his father, "I'm not giving you a horse. You don't know how to talk. No, it's your brothers who are the clever fellows."

"If I can't have a horse," said Booby Jack, "I'll take the billy-goat; it's my own and I can

ride it." And, sitting astride the goat, he dug his heels into its sides and raced off up the road. Whew, how it ran! "Here I come!" cried Booby Jack, singing out till the echoes rang.

But his brothers rode ahead in silence. Neither of them spoke, they were thinking over all the good ideas they were going to talk about, for they intended to be very artful.

"Ahoy, ahoy!" shouted Booby Jack, "here I come, look what I've found in the road!" And he showed them a dead crow he had found.

"Booby!" they said, "what do you want with that?"

"I'm going to present it to the king's daughter."

"You do that," they said, and with a laugh they rode on.

"Ahoy! Here I come, look what I've got now, you don't find things like this in the road every day of the week!" The brothers turned once again to see what he had found. "Booby!" they said, "that's just an old clog with the top missing, is that for the king's daughter too?"

"Yes, it is," said Booby Jack, and his brothers laughed and rode on until they were far ahead.

"Ahoy! Here I am," shouted Booby Jack. "Oh, it gets better and better, ahoy! This takes the prize."

"What have you found now?" said his brothers, "Oh," said Booby Jack, "it's impossible to say how pleased she'll be, that princess."

"Ugh!" said the brothers, "that's mud thrown up from the ditch."

"Yes, so it is," said Booby Jack, "and it's the very finest quality, you can't even hold it," and he filled his pockets with the mud.

The brothers rode for all they were worth until they were a full hour ahead. Then they stopped at the city gates, where the suitors were given numbers according to their order of arrival and were drawn up six to a row and packed so tightly that they could not move their arms, which was a very good thing because otherwise they would have sliced each other up just because some were ahead of the others.

All the rest of the population were crowded round the castle, right up to the windows, to watch the princess receiving her suitors, but as soon as one came into the room there was an end to his eloquence.

"No good!" said the princess. "Out!"

In came the brother who knew the dictionary, but he had completely forgotten it while he was standing in line, and the floor creaked and the ceiling was made of mirror-glass so that he saw himself upside down and at every window stood three clerks and a guildsman, each writing down everything that was said so that it could go straight in to the newspapers and be sold on the street corner for twopence. This was terrible; and then the stove had been stoked so fiercely that it glowed red.

"It's terribly hot in here," said the suitor.

"That's because my father is roasting cocks today," said the princess.

"Bah!" There he stood, taken aback by her words and without a single one of his own, although he had meant to say something witty.

"No good!" said the princess. "Out!" And he had to go. In came the second brother.

"The heat's awful in here!" he said.

"Yes, we're roasting cocks today," said the king's daughter.

"What do – what?" he said, and all the clerks wrote down: *What do – what?*

"No good!" said the princess. "Out!"

In came Booby Jack, riding his billy-goat right into the hall. "It's burning hot in here!" he said.

"That's because I'm roasting cocks," said the king's daughter.

"What a good idea," said Booby Jack, "You could roast me a crow, then?"

"You can roast your crow," said the king's daughter, "but I hope you have something to roast it in, for I have neither pot nor pan."

"But I have!" said Booby Jack. "Here's a cooking pot with a pewter staple," and taking out the old clog, he put the crow in it.

"That's enough for a meal," said the king's daughter, "but where's the sauce coming from?"

"I've got it in my pocket," said Booby Jack. "I've got so much that I can afford to waste it," and he poured a little mud out of his pocket.

"I like this!" said the king's daughter, "you can answer back, and you can speak up, and I'm going to marry you! But did you know that every word we say, and every word we've already said, is being written down and will be in the newspaper tomorrow? There are three clerks and an old guild-master at every window and the guild-master is the worst because he doesn't understand."

She said that to frighten him and all the clerks whinnied and splashed ink on the floor.

"What a grand lot!" said Booby Jack. "Then I'll give the old man the best!" And turning out his pockets he let the old man have the mud right in the face.

"That was well done," said the king's daughter. "I could not have done that, but I shall soon learn!"

So Booby Jack became king, gained a wife and a crown and sat on a throne, and we got the story straight from the guild-master's newspaper – which is not to be trusted.

# The Emperor's New Clothes

Many years ago there lived an emperor who was so tremendously fond of smart new clothes that he spent all his money on being well dressed. He gave no thought to his soldiers nor to the theatre nor to driving in the woods; all he cared about was showing off his new clothes. He had a costume for every hour of the day and just as they say of a king that he is "in council", so, in that country, they always said: "The emperor is in his wardrobe."

In the great city where he lived, life was very enjoyable; many visitors arrived every day, and one day two swindlers came to town. They claimed to be weavers and said that they could weave the most beautiful cloth imaginable. It was not only the colours and the pattern which were unusually elegant, but the clothes made out of the cloth had the remarkable property of being invisible to anyone who was unfit for his office or outrageously stupid.

"Those must be wonderful clothes," thought the emperor. "If I were wearing them I should

soon find out which men in my kingdom are unfit for their office, I should know who was wise and who was stupid – yes, I must have that cloth woven for me at once!" He gave the two swindlers a great deal of money in advance so that they could begin on their work.

They actually set up two looms and pretended to be working, but there was nothing at all on the looms. They called boldly for the finest silk and purest gold which they popped into their pockets and went on working on the empty looms, even late at night.

"I would dearly like to know how much cloth they've woven," thought the emperor, but in fact it made him hesitate a little when he remembered that anyone who was stupid or not worthy of his position would not be able to see the cloth. Of course, he didn't think there was any need for him to worry, but all the same, he decided to send someone ahead to see how things were going. All the people in the city knew of the cloth's miraculous powers and they were all eager to see how incompetent or stupid their neighbours were.

"I shall send my honest old minister to see the weavers," thought the emperor. "He'll be able to see what the cloth looks like, because he's an intelligent man and no one fits his post better than he."

Off went the good-natured old minister to the room where the two swindlers were still working on the empty loom. "God bless us and save us!" thought the old minister, opening his eyes wide, "I can't see anything at all." But he did not say so.

The two swindlers asked him to be so good as to come closer and demanded to know if the pattern was not charming and the colours beautiful. They pointed at the empty loom and the poor old minister went on stretching his eyes, but he could see nothing, for there was nothing there. "Good Lord!" he thought, "does it mean I'm stupid? I have never thought so, and no one must know it. Am I unfit for my office? No, I must certainly not tell anyone that I can't see the cloth!"

"Well, have you nothing to say?" said the one who was weaving.

"Oh, it's charming, perfectly adorable," said the old minister, peering through his glasses, "that pattern and those colours – yes, I shall tell the emperor that I am quite particularly pleased."

"Well, we're delighted," said the two weavers, beginning to describe the colours and the unique pattern. The old minister listened carefully in order to say the same thing when he reported to the emperor.

The swindlers now demanded more money and more silk and gold for the weaving. They put it all in their own pockets and not a single thread reached the loom, but they continued to weave on the empty loom as before.

Soom the emperor sent off another amiable official to see how the weaving was going and whether the cloth would soon be ready. Like the minister, the official stared and stared, but since there was nothing there but the empty loom, he could see nothing.

"Well, isn't it an attractive piece of cloth?" said the two weavers, pointing and explaining the beautiful pattern which was not there at all.

"I'm not stupid," thought the official, "so I must be unfit for my excellent post. That seems rather odd, but I mustn't let anyone know." So he praised the cloth he could not see and assured them of his pleasure at the pretty colours and the beautiful pattern. "Yes, it's absolutely delightful," he told the emperor.

Everyone in the city was talking about the wonderful cloth.

Now the emperor himself decided to see it while it was still on the loom. With a whole crowd of distinguished people, including the two nice old officials who had already been there, he went to see the two cunning swindlers who were now weaving with might and main, but not with silken thread.

"Well, isn't it magnificent?" said the two amiable officials. "Will Your Majesty deign to look, such patterns, such colours!" And they pointed to the empty loom, because they believed the others would be able to see the cloth.

"What's this!" thought the emperor, "I can see nothing, this is terrible, am I stupid? Am I unfit to be the emperor? That would be the most awful thing that could happen to me."

"Oh, it's most attractive," he said, "it has my absolute approval." And he nodded with satisfaction, looking at the empty loom. He had no intention of saying that he could see nothing. The whole company stared and stared, getting no more out of it than anyone else, yet, like the emperor, they said: "Oh, it's most attractive!" and they advised him to have this new, splendid cloth made into clothes to be worn for the first time in the next great procession. "It's magnificent, so dainty, excellent!" The words passed from mouth to mouth, everyone was simply delighted. The emperor gave both swindlers a ribbon to wear in their buttonholes and the title of Knight of the Loom.

The swindlers sat up all night before the

morning of the procession, using more than sixteen candles so that people could see how busy they were, making up the emperor's new clothes. They pretended to be taking the cloth off the loom, they snipped at the air with huge scissors and sewed with unthreaded needles, until at last: "Look, the clothes are ready!" they said.

The emperor himself arrived with his noble courtiers and the two swindlers raised one arm each as if they were holding something, saying: "Look, here are the trousers! Here is the robe! And here is the cloak!" And so on, and so on. "The cloth is as light as gossamer, you simply can't feel it on your body, but that's the virtue of it."

"Yes!" said all the courtiers, but they could see nothing, for there was nothing there.

"Now if Your Imperial Majesty will be gracious enough to remove your clothes," said the swindlers, "we will fit the new ones on you in front of the big mirror."

The emperor took off all his clothes and the swindlers pretended to be handing him the new ones they had made, one at a time, putting their arms around him and appearing to tie on what was supposed to be the train, while the emperor twisted and turned before the mirror.

"Lord, how they suit you, how beautifully they fit!" said everybody. "What a pattern! What colours! Oh, what precious robes!"

"They are waiting outside with the canopy to be carried over Your Majesty's head in the procession," said the master of ceremonies.

"Well, I'm quite ready," said the emperor. "Don't they fit well?" He turned round yet again in front of the mirror, trying to look as if he were considering his finery.

The lords-in-waiting who were to carry the train fumbled about on the floor as if they were picking it up. They walked along, holding their hands up, not daring to let anyone know that they could see nothing.

Then the emperor walked in the procession under the beautiful canopy and all the people in the streets and at their windows said: "Lord,

how superb the emperor's new clothes look! What a beautiful train he has on his robe, how perfectly it fits!" No one intended to reveal that he could see nothing, for in that case he was either unfit for his office or very stupid. None of the emperor's clothes had ever been so successful.

"But he hasn't got anything on!" said a little

child. "Good Lord, out of the mouths of babes!" said his father and each one whispered to the next what the child had said.

"He's got nothing on! A little child said he's got nothing on!"

"He's got nothing on!" the whole crowd roared at last, and the emperor shuddered, for it seemed to him that they were right, but he thought: "I shall have to go through with the procession." So he bore himself even more proudly and the lords-in-waiting went on holding up the train which was not there at all.

# The Wild Swans

Far away from here, where the swallows go when we have winter, there lived a king who had eleven sons and one daughter, Elisa. The eleven brothers, all princes, went to school with a star on their chest and a sword at their side; they wrote on golden tablets with diamond pencils and they read so well, both aloud and silently, that you could tell at once they were princes. Their sister Elisa sat on a little stool made of mirror-glass with her picture-book, which had cost half the kingdom.

Those children had wonderful lives, but things would not always be so.

Their father, who ruled over the whole country, married a wicked queen, which was very bad for the poor children; they realized that on the very first day, when there was great pomp and ceremony throughout the castle and the children played at tea-parties, for instead of having all the cake and baked apples they could eat, in the usual way, their stepmother gave them nothing but sand in a tea-cup, and told them to pretend it was something else.

The next week she put their little sister Elisa out in the country to live with a peasant family and it was not long before she had made the king believe so many things about the poor

96

princes that he no longer cared for them.

"Fly out into the world and fend for yourselves!" said the wicked queen, "fly, like birds with no voice!" But she was unable to do all the ill she wished, for they became eleven beautiful wild swans and uttering a strange call they flew out of the castle windows across the park and the forest.

It was still quite early in the morning when they passed the place where their sister Elisa lay asleep in the peasant's cottage; they hovered over the roof, twisting their long necks and beating their wings, but no one heard or saw them; they had to go on, high up in the clouds, far out into the wide world. They flew to a great, dark forest which stretched right down to the water's edge.

Poor little Elisa in the peasant's hut played with a green leaf for want of any other toys. She made a hole in the leaf and peeped through it at the sun and imagined that she could see her brothers' bright eyes and every time the warm rays touched her cheek she thought of all their kisses.

Day after monotonous day passed. When the wind blew through the tall rose hedge outside the house it whispered to the roses: "Who could be lovelier than you?" and the roses tossed their heads and said: "Elisa!" And when the old woman sat in the doorway of a Sunday, reading her prayer book, the wind ruffled the leaves: "Who could be more pious than you?" it asked. "Elisa!" said the prayer book, and what the roses and the prayer book said was true.

When she was fifteen years old she was supposed to return home but when the queen saw how pretty she was she was filled with anger and hatred and would gladly have turned her into a wild swan like her brothers, but she dared not do it at once, for the king wanted to see his daughter.

Early next morning the queen went to her bathroom, which was built of marble and adorned with soft cushions and beautiful carpets. She took three toads, kissed them, and said to the first: "Sit on Elisa's head when she gets into the bath so that she becomes as lumpish as you! And you," she said to the second, "sit on her forehead so that she becomes as ugly as you and her father does not recognize her! Lie close to her heart," she whispered to the third, "and give her an evil disposition that will torment her!" She put the toads into the clean water, which at once took on a greenish colour, called to Elisa, undressed her and told her to get into the water. As she lay down one of the toads climbed into her hair, another onto her forehead, and the third onto her breast, but Elisa seemed not to notice them at all and when she stood up there were three red poppies floating on the water. Had the creatures not been poisonous and kissed by the witch, they would have turned into red roses, but they became flowers anyway by lying on her head and close to her heart; she was too pure and innocent for their magic to have any power over her.

When the wicked queen saw this she rubbed her with walnut juice until she was blackish-brown all over and streaked her pretty face with a stinking ointment and tangled her lovely hair until Elisa's beauty was unrecognizable.

When her father saw her he was very startled and said she was not his daughter; no one knew her but the watchdog and the swallows, but they were only animals and no one listened to them. Poor Elisa wept and thought of her eleven brothers, who had all gone. She stole sadly out of the castle and walked all day through marsh and meadow into the great forest. She had no idea where she was going, but she felt very sad and longed to see her brothers who, like her, had been banished into the wide world, and she was determined to find them.

Night fell before she had been long in the forest; she had completely lost sight of the path, so she lay down on the soft moss, said her evening prayers and pillowed her head on a stump. It was very quiet, the air was soft and all around her in the grass and on the moss hundreds of fireflies shone like green fire; when

she touched a branch gently with her hand the shining insects fell about her like shooting stars.

All night she dreamed about her brothers; they were playing together, writing with diamond pencils on golden tablets and looking at the beautiful picture-book which had cost half the kingdom, as before, but now they no longer drew noughts and crosses on the tablets, oh no, they drew all their daring exploits and the many things they had seen and done; the picture-book came alive, the birds sang and the people came out of the book and talked to Elisa and her brothers, but when she turned the page they jumped in again, so that the pictures would not be in the wrong order.

When she woke up the sun was already high in the sky. In fact she could not see it because the branches of the trees were so thickly intertwined, but the sunbeams were playing among them in a shifting golden haze; the leaves were fragrant and the birds were quite happy to settle on her shoulders. She heard water splashing from many springs, which all ran out into a pool with a nice, sandy bottom; it was thickly surrounded by bushes, but in one place the deer had nibbled a wide opening and through it Elisa went down to the water which was so clear that, had a breeze not stirred the bushes and branches, she would have thought they were painted on the bottom, so distinctly was every leaf reflected, whether it lay in sunshine or in shadow.

99

When she saw her own face she was terribly startled, it was so brown and hideous, but after she had rubbed her eyes and forehead with handfuls of water the white skin shone through again, so she took off all her clothes and walked into the clear water – there was never a more beautiful princess in all the world.

When she had dressed herself and plaited her long hair she drank water from the sparkling spring, in the hollow of her hand, and wandered deeper into the forest without knowing where she was going. She thought of her brothers, she thought of the good Lord, who would surely not desert her; He made the wild apples grow to feed the hungry; He showed her a tree, its branches bowed down with fruit, where she ate her midday meal, set up props to support the branches and walked on into the darkest part of the forest. The silence was so deep that she could hear her own footsteps and the sound of every withered leaf that crackled beneath her feet. There was not a bird to be seen, not a single ray of sunshine could penetrate the great inter-laced branches; the tall trunks were so close together that when she looked ahead she seemed to be enclosed by a fence of close-set posts. Oh, how lonely she was, lonelier than she had ever been before!

The night was very dark, not a single firefly glimmered on the moss as she lay sadly down to sleep. But then the branches above her seemed to part, Our Lord's gentle eyes were looking down on her and little angels clustered about His head. When she woke up next morning she did not know if she had been dreaming or if it had really happened.

She had walked only a little way when she met an old woman with a basket of berries; the old woman gave her some and Elisa asked if she had seen eleven princes riding through the forest.

"No," said the old woman, "but yesterday I saw eleven swans with golden crowns on their heads swimming down the stream nearby."

She led Elisa to a cliff at whose foot there ran a winding stream. The trees on its banks stretched out their long, leafy branches towards each other and where they could not reach each other by their natural growth they had tugged their roots out of the ground and leaned out over the water to intertwine their branches.

Elisa said goodbye to the old woman and walked along the stream to where it ran out over the open beach.

All the beauty of the sea now lay before the young girl, but there was not a sail to be seen, nor a boat in which she could have travelled further. She looked at the countless pebbles on the shore, all rounded by the waves. Glass, iron, stone, all the flotsam and jetsam had been shaped by the water, although it was far softer even than her delicate hand. "You roll and roll and never tire and the hardest things are smoothed. I shall become as tireless as you! Thank you for your lesson, you clear, rolling waves. One day, my heart tells me, you will carry me to my dear brothers."

In the seaweed washed up on the beach lay eleven white swan's feathers, which she collected in a bunch. Drops of water hung on them but she could not see if they·were dew or tears. It was lonely on the shore, but she did not feel it because the sea was constantly changing, changing more in a few hours than fresh-water lakes do in a whole year. When black clouds passed overhead the sea seemed to be saying: "I can look dark, too," and then the wind blew and the waves were tipped with white. But if the clouds were red and the wind slept the sea was like a rose petal; it would turn now green, now white, but however still it lay, there was always some slight movement on the shore; the water lifted gently, like the breast of a sleeping child.

Just before sunset Elisa saw eleven wild swans with gold crowns on their heads flying inland, gliding one behind the other. Climbing the cliff, Elisa hid herself behind a bush; the swans settled near her and flapped their great white wings.

When the sun had sunk beneath the water the swan skins suddenly fell off and there stood

eleven handsome princes, Elisa's brothers. She uttered a loud cry, because although they had changed so much she knew who they were; she felt that they must be her brothers, and running into their arms, she called them by name. They were all overjoyed when they saw and recognized their little sister, who was now so tall and beautiful. They laughed and cried as they realized how wicked their step-mother had been to them all.

"We brothers," the eldest told her, "fly about as wild swans as long as the sun is in the sky. When it sets we take on our human form, that is why we must always be careful to have firm ground under our feet at sunset, for, if we were flying among the clouds, we would plunge to the ground as we became human beings. We don't live here; there is another land as beautiful as this on the other side of the sea, but it is a long way off, we have to cross the ocean, and there are no islands on the way where we can spend the night, only a lonely little rock which stands up out of the sea. It is just big enough for us to rest on side by side and when the sea is high the water sprays over our heads, yet we thank God for it. There we spend the night in our human form; without it we could never visit our homeland, because we spend two of the longest days in the year on our flight. We are able to visit our home only once a year and to remain for eleven days, flying over this great forest from which we can see the castle where we were born and where our father lives. We can see the tall tower of the church by which Mother lies buried. Here we feel that the trees and bushes are kindred, here the wild horses race across the plains as they did in our childhood; here the charcoal-burners sing the old songs we danced to as children, this is our homeland, which draws us back, and here we have found you, our dear little sister! We can stay here for only two more days, then we must fly across the sea to the beautiful country which is not our homeland: how can we take you with us? We have neither boat nor ship!"

"How can I break the spell that binds you?"

said their sister.

They talked nearly all night, sleeping for only a short time.

Elisa was awakened by the sound of the swans' wings rushing over her head. Her brothers had changed shape again and were flying, first in great circles and then further away, but one of them, the youngest, stayed with her, laying its head in her lap, and she stroked its white wings. They were together all day long.

Towards evening the others returned and when the sun set they resumed their natural form.

"Tomorrow we must fly away and we dare not return for a whole year, but we cannot abandon you like this. Have you the courage to come with us? My arms are strong enough to carry you through the forest, would our wings not be strong enough to carry you across the sea?"

"Yes, take me with you!" said Elisa.

They spent the night weaving a net from the pliant willow bark and the tough rushes until it was big and strong enough. Elisa lay down on it and when the sun rose and her brothers turned into white swans they took the net in their beaks and flew high among the clouds with their dear sister, still sleeping. The sun's rays were shining on her face, so one of the swans flew above her head, shading her with his broad wings.

They were far from land when Elisa woke up, still dreaming, she thought, astonished by the strangeness of being carried across the sea, high in the air. At her side lay a branch covered with ripe berries and a bunch of tasty roots which her youngest brother had gathered for her. She smiled her thanks to him, because she knew it was he who was flying just above her head, shading her with his wings.

They were flying so high that the first ship they saw beneath them looked like a white gull floating on the water. There was a great cloud behind them, as big as a mountain, and on it Elisa saw the shadows of herself and the eleven

swans. The flying shadows were gigantic, they made a picture more wonderful than any she had seen before, but as the sun rose higher and the clouds lay further behind them, so the shifting shadow picture disappeared.

All day they flew through the air like one speeding arrow, yet they travelled less swiftly now that they had their sister to carry. A storm blew up as evening drew near and Elisa was troubled as she saw the sun going down the sky before that lonely rock was in sight. She realized that the swans were beating their wings more desperately. It was her fault that they could not travel fast enough: when the sun had set they would turn into human beings, fall into the sea and drown. She prayed from the depths of her soul to Our Lord, but still she could see no rock; the black cloud drew nearer and the strong gusts heralded a storm. Now the clouds formed a solid, threatening wave, moving forward like a sheet of lead; one lightning flash followed another. The sun had reached the horizon and Elisa's heart failed her as the swans plunged downward, so fast that she thought they were falling, but in a moment they were gliding again. The sun was half in the water when she suddenly saw the little rock beneath them, looking no bigger than a seal poking its head out of the water. The sun was sinking fast, it was little more than a star now and as her foot touched firm ground, the sun's light was quenched like the burning spark from a scrap of paper; she saw her brothers standing round her, arm-in-arm, but there was scarcely room for herself and them. The sea burst against the rock, showering them like rain; the sky was one continuous burning flame and the crash of thunder went on and on, but sister and brothers stood hand-in-hand, singing a hymn which gave them courage and confidence.

At dawn the sky was clear and still and as soon as the sun rose the swans flew off again with Elisa. The sea was still stormy and when they rose higher the white foam on the dark green waves looked like millions of swans floating on the water.

When the sun was higher Elisa saw before her, as if hanging in the air, a mountainous countryside, its fields covered with shining ice and in the middle of it a mile-long castle with one soaring colonnade above another; beneath it swayed palm trees and exotic flowers as big as mill wheels. She asked if this were the country they were going to, but the swans shook their heads. This, she now saw, was the beautiful, ever-changing cloud-castle of Fata Morgana, which no man must enter. Elisa stared at it; then mountains, trees and castle vanished and there stood twenty proud churches, with high towers and pointed windows. She thought she heard an organ playing, but it was only the sea. When she was quite close to the churches they turned into a fleet of ships sailing beneath her; she looked down and they were nothing but wisps of fog blowing over the water. She watched the ever-changing scene until she saw the real country she was going to, splendid blue mountains and cedar forests, towns and castles. Long before the sun had set she was sitting in front of a big cave hung with slender green climbing plants which looked like embroidered tapestries.

"Now let's see what you dream in here tonight!" said her youngest brother, showing her to her bedroom.

"If only I could dream how to release you!" she said, and the thought filled her mind; she prayed to God with all her heart to help her, and even in her sleep her prayers went on. Then she seemed to be floating high in the air to the cloud palace of Fata Morgana and the fairy came to meet her, grand and glittering, yet very like the old woman who had given her berries in the wood and told her of the swans wearing golden crowns.

"Your brothers can be freed," she said, "but have you courage and endurance enough? The sea water is softer than your delicate hands and yet it reshapes the hard stone, but it does not feel the pain your fingers would feel; it has no heart and cannot suffer the fear and torment which you must bear. Do you see this stinging

nettle in my hand? There are many of these round the cave where you are sleeping, only those and the ones that grow round the church-yard will do, remember that. You must pick them, although they make your skin burn and blister; tread the nettles into flax with your feet, twine thread from it and make eleven knitted shirts with long sleeves, throw them over the eleven wild swans and the spell will be broken. But remember, from the moment that you begin your work until it is completed, even if it takes years, you must not speak; the first word you utter will pierce your brothers' hearts like a dagger; their lives depend on your tongue. Mark this well!''

So saying, she touched Elisa's hand with the nettle, which burned like fire, waking her up. It was daylight and close by her sleeping place lay a nettle like the one she had seen in her dream. She fell on her knees, thanking God, and left the cave to start work. With her delicate hands she pulled up the hideous, fiery nettles which burned great blisters on her hands and arms, but she was happy to bear them if only she could release her dear brothers. She trampled each nettle with her tender feet and twined the green flax into threads.

After sunset her brothers arrived and were frightened by her silence, believing it to be a new spell cast by their wicked step-mother, but when they saw her hands they understood what she was doing for them. The youngest brother wept and where his tears fell she felt no pain and the burning blisters disappeared.

She spent all night working, unable to sleep until she had released her dear brothers. All the next day, while the swans were gone, she sat alone, but time had never passed so quickly. One knitted shirt was already finished and she began on the second.

Then the sound of a hunting horn rang through the mountains, startling her. The sound came closer until she could hear the hounds barking, and hurrying fearfully into the cave she tied up the nettles she had gathered and trodden in a bundle and sat on it.

At that moment a hound came bounding out of the thicket, and then another and then another; they barked loudly and ran to and fro. In a few minutes all the huntsmen were standing outside the cave and the handsomest of them was that country's king. He had never seen a more beautiful girl than Elisa, and he went to her.

"How did you get here, you lovely child?" he said. Elisa shook her head, not daring to speak since it would cost her brothers their freedom and their lives. She hid her hands under her apron too, so that the king should not see what she suffered.

"Come with me," he said, "you must not stay here, and if you are as good as you are beautiful I shall clothe you in silk and velvet and put a golden crown on your head and my richest palace shall be your dwelling place!" So saying, he lifted her onto his horse, though she wept and wrung her hands. "I want only your happiness," said the king, "one day you will thank me!" And he rode off across the mountains, holding her in front of him, with the huntsmen following on behind.

When the sun went down they reached the splendid royal city with its churches and domes and the king led her into the castle where great fountains splashed in high marble halls, where walls and ceilings were resplendent with paintings, but she had no eyes for them. She wept and mourned, allowing the women to clothe her in royal blue robes and not resisting as they braided her hair with pearls and drew thin gloves over her blistered fingers.

Standing there in all her finery she was so dazzlingly beautiful that the court bowed to her even more deeply than usual and the king chose her as his bride, although the archbishop shook his head and whispered that the pretty girl from the woods was a witch, who had bedazzled their eyes and bewitched the king's heart.

But the king paid no attention, ordered the musicians to play, the most costly dishes to be presented, and the most graceful girls to dance for her. She was led through fragrant gardens

into splendid rooms, but no smile touched her lips or reached her eyes; her grief seemed to have been imprinted there for ever. Then the king opened a little room where she was to sleep; it had been decorated with precious green tapestries and made to look exactly like the cave she had been living in; on the floor lay the bundle of flax she had spun from the nettles and from the ceiling hung the shirts she had already knitted; they had been collected by one of the huntsmen as a curiosity.

"You can dream yourself back to your former home here," said the king. "Here is the work you were doing and now in all your new splendour it will entertain you to remember those days."

When Elisa saw the things that were so close to her heart there was a hint of a smile on her lips and the blood returned to her cheeks; remembering her brothers' freedom, she kissed the king's hand and he pressed her to his heart and ordered all the church bells to announce the wedding feast. The beautiful, silent girl from the forest was the country's queen.

The archbishop whispered evil words in the king's ear, but they failed to reach his heart: the marriage should proceed, the archbishop himself must place the crown on her head, and with an ill-will he pushed the band tightly over her forehead so that it hurt her. Yet round her heart lay the heavier band of grief for her brothers; she was unaware of the physical pain. Her mouth was dumb, for a single word would end her brothers' lives, but in her eyes lay a deep love for the kind, handsome king who did all he could to please her. She grew fonder of him day by day and longed with all her heart to confide in him, tell him of her suffering, but she must complete her work in silence. So every night she stole from his side to the little powder closet decorated like her cave and knitted one shift after another; but when she began on the seventh she had no more flax.

She knew that the nettles she needed were growing in the churchyard, but she would have to pick them herself: how was she to go there?

"Oh, what is the pain in my fingers against the torment of my heart!" she thought. "I must be brave! God will protect me." As deeply troubled as if she were planning some wickedness, she stole into the garden in the bright moonlight, walked down the long avenues and out into the lonely streets to the churchyard. There, on one of the broadest gravestones, sat a circle of lamias, blood-sucking serpent witches, and as she passed close by them they fixed their evil eyes on her, but, praying silently, she gathered the burning nettles and bore them home to the castle.

Only one person had seen her, the archbishop, who had stayed awake while the others slept. He had been right after all! The queen was not all she should be: she was a witch, who had cast her spell over the king and all his people.

In the confessional he told the king what he had seen and what he feared and as the harsh words left his tongue the carved images of saints shook their heads as if to say: "That is wrong, Elisa is innocent," but the archbishop gave a different explanation, saying that they were bearing witness against her and shaking their heads over her sins. Two heavy tears ran down the king's cheeks and he went home with doubt in his heart. That night he pretended to sleep, but no sleep visited his eyes; he was aware of Elisa getting up, night after night, and night after night he followed her and saw her going to her powder closet.

Day by day his expression grew sterner, but though Elisa noticed, she did not know why. All the same, it troubled her and coupled with her suffering for her brothers, it made her weep salt tears on her royal velvet and purple, which winked like diamonds, so that everyone who saw her rich finery wished they could be queen. Not long afterwards, her work was nearly finished. There was only one more shirt to be made, but she had no flax left and not a single nettle. Just once more, for the last time, she would have to go to the churchyard and pick a few handfuls. She thought distressfully of the

lonely walk and the dreadful lamias, but her will was as firm as her trust in the Lord.

Elisa went, but the king and the archbishop followed her and watched her passing through the wrought iron gate into the churchyard and, as they approached, they saw the lamias that Elisa had seen sitting on the gravestone and the king turned away, because he imagined that in their midst was she whose head had rested on his breast that very evening.

"The people must judge her," he said, and the people's judgment was that she should be burned at the stake.

She was taken from the magnificent royal hall to a dark dungeon where the wind whistled in at the barred window; instead of silks and velvet they gave her the bundle of nettles she had gathered as a pillow and the bitter, burning shirts she had knitted for her only quilt and blanket, but they could have given her nothing more precious. She started work again, praying to God.

Outside her prison the urchins sang derisive ditties about her; there was not a soul to comfort her with a loving word.

Then, towards evening, a swan's wing brushed past the bars: it was her youngest brother who had found her and she sobbed aloud for joy, although she knew that the coming night might be the last she had to live. But her work was nearly finished too, and her brothers were there.

The archbishop came to spend her last hours with her as he had promised the king, but she shook her head and begged him with looks and gestures to leave her: her work must be finished that night, otherwise it would all have been in vain, all her pain, her tears and sleepless nights. The archbishop left her with angry words, but poor Elisa knew that she was innocent and went on with her work.

The little mice ran across the floor, dragging the nettles to her feet, to help her, and the thrush sat by the bars singing the whole night through, as cheerfully as it could, to give her courage.

It was scarcely dawn, an hour before sunrise, when her eleven brothers arrived at the castle gate, demanding to see the king. Not so, came the answer, it was still night, the king was asleep and must not be wakened. They begged and threatened until the guard came and the king himself came out to find out what was going on. At that very moment the sun rose and instead of eleven brothers, eleven wild swans were flying above the castle.

All the inhabitants of the town streamed out to watch the burning of the witch. A wretched nag pulled the cart she was sitting in. She had been given a coarse sackcloth shift to wear, her beautiful long hair hung loose round her lovely face, her cheeks were deathly pale and her lips moved softly, but her fingers still worked at the green flax. Even going to her death she did not

give up the work she had begun; ten shirts lay at her feet and she was still knitting the eleventh.

The people mocked her: "Look at the witch mumbling! She's got no prayer book, she's weaving her loathsome spells, get it away from her, tear it to bits!"

Crowding round her they tried to tear her work away, but eleven white swans flew down, settled all round her on the cart and beat their great wings so that the frightened mob had to give way.

"It is a sign from heaven, she must be innocent!" many of them whispered, but they did not dare to repeat it aloud.

As the hangman reached for her hand she hastily threw the eleven shirts over the swans and there stood eleven handsome princes, but the youngest had one swan's wing instead of an arm because one sleeve was still missing from his shirt, which she had not had time to finish.

"Now I dare speak!" she said: "I am innocent!"

And the people, seeing what had happened, bowed before her as if to a saint, but Elisa swooned in her brothers' arms, worn out with suspense, anxiety and pain.

"Yes, she is innocent!" said her eldest brother and he told the whole story. As he spoke there arose a fragrance as of a million roses, for the wood piled round the stake had taken root and put out branches, becoming a fragrant hedge, very high and thick and covered with red roses. At the very top a single, radiant white flower shone like a star. The king plucked it and laid it on Elisa's breast and she awakened with peace and joy in her heart.

Then all the church bells rang out of their own accord, all the birds of the air came flocking in and the wedding procession back to the castle was finer than any king had seen until that day.

# Father's Always Right

Now I'm going to tell you a story I heard when I was a little boy and, every time I have remembered it since, it seems to have got even nicer, for stories are like many people, they get nicer and nicer as they grow old, and that's delightful!

You must have been out in the country sometime and, if so, you may have seen a really old house with a thatched roof; moss and weeds grow on the thatch and there is a stork's nest on the ridge; you can't do without the stork. The walls are crooked, the windows low, in fact there is only one that opens properly. The baking oven pouts out like a fat little tummy and the elderberry bush leans over the fence. There is a little pond and a duck with ducklings, bobbing under the gnarled willow tree. Yes, and of course there is a watchdog which barks at all and sundry.

It was in just such a house as this that there lived two people, a farmer and his wife. Little as they had, there was one thing they could not do without and that was a horse, which grazed on the road verges. Father rode it into town,

the neighbours borrowed it and he received favour for favour – but it might be even more favourable for him to sell the horse or exchange it for something else which would be even more useful to them both. But what should it be?

"You know best about that, Father," said his wife. "It's market day in town, you ride in and sell the horse for money or make a good exchange. Whatever you do is always right. You ride to market!"

She tied his neckcloth herself, for she did it better than he could, giving him a double bow to make him look more dashing. Then she brushed his hat with the flat of her hand, kissed him on his warm mouth and off he rode on the horse which was to be sold or exchanged. Oh yes, that was Father's business.

The sun was shining, there was not a cloud in the sky. The road was dusty with all the market people going in by horse or carriage or on their own two feet. It was burning hot and there was not a single bit of shade on the road.

There was a man walking along with a cow just as pretty as a cow can be. "That must give good milk," thought the farmer, "it might be a very good idea to make an exchange."

"Look here, you with the cow," he said, "let's have a little talk! Now, it's my belief that a horse costs more than a cow, but never mind, a cow would be more use to me: shall we exchange?"

"Why not!" said the man with the cow, and they made the exchange.

Now it was done and the farmer could have gone home again, having done what he intended, but having once decided to go to the market he would go to the market, just to have a look. So on he went with his cow. He walked fast and the cow walked fast and they soon caught up with a man leading a sheep. It was a good sheep, stout and with a good fleece.

"I'd like to own that," thought the farmer. "There would be no lack of grazing for it on our verges and in winter we could take it into the room with us. It would really be better for us to keep a sheep than a cow. Shall we exchange?"

The man with the sheep was perfectly willing, so the exchange was made and the farmer went on walking down the road with his sheep. Soon he saw a man standing by a stile with a big goose under his arm.

"That's a heavy one you've got there," said the farmer. "It's got feathers and fat in plenty. That would look well on a tether by our pond and it would be something for Mother to collect her peelings for. She was just saying 'If only we had a goose!' Now she can have one – and she shall have one! Will you exchange? I'll give you the sheep for the goose and my thanks into the bargain!"

The other man was quite willing and they made the exchange: the farmer got the goose. He was close to the town now, the crowds on the road were increasing, until it was teeming with men and beasts. They walked all over the road and on the roadside and on to the gate-keeper's potato patch where his chicken was tied up so that it would not run off in a fright and get lost. It was a short-tailed hen which winked an eye and looked agreeable. "Cluck, cluck!" it said, and what it was thinking I cannot say, but the farmer thought when he saw it: she's the most beautiful hen I've ever seen, even better than the minister's broody hen, I'd like to own that! A chicken always finds some grain, it can almost fend for itself, so I believe it would be a good exchange to give up the goose for it.

"Shall we exchange?" he asked. "Exchange?" said the other, "yes, that's not a bad idea!" And they made the exchange. The gatekeeper got the goose, the farmer got the hen.

By now he had done a great deal on his journey into town; it was hot and he was tired. A dram and a bite of bread were what he needed and when he reached the inn he decided to go inside, but in the doorway he met the ostler coming out with a bulging sack.

"What have you got there?" he asked.

"Rotten apples!" said the man, "a whole sackful for the pigs."

"That's an awful lot! I'd like Mother to see that, for last year we had only the one apple on the old tree by the peat shed. That one was put away carefully and it stayed in the chest-of-drawers until it burst. 'It's still a bit of riches,' Mother said. This would give her a sight of real riches! Yes, I'd like her to have this."

"Well, what will you give me?" asked the ostler.

"Give you? I'll give you my hen in exchange." So he handed over the hen, took the apples and went up to the counter to order a drink. He propped his sack of apples against the stove, which was lit, but he did not think of that. There were a great many strangers in the tap-room, horse dealers, cattle dealers and two Englishmen so rich that their pockets were bursting with gold. They loved a gamble, as you will soon hear!

Hiss! Hiss! What was that noise from the stove? The apples were beginning to bake!

"What's that?" asked the rich man. They were soon being told the whole story of the horse that had been exchanged for a cow and right on down to the rotten apples.

"Well, Mother's going to cuff you when you get home!" said the Englishmen, "you'll have the house round your ears!"

"I'll get a kiss, not a cuff," said the farmer. "Mother will say: Father's always right!"

"Let's have a bet," said they, "we'll wager a barrelful of gold coin!"

"A bushelful will be enough," said the farmer, "and I can only wager the bushel of apples with Mother and me thrown in, but that's more than a level measure, it's a heaped measure!"

"Done! Done!" said they, and so the bet was made.

The innkeeper's carriage was brought out, the Englishmen got in, the farmer got in, the rotten apples got in and soon they were at the farmer's house.

"Good evening, Mother."

"Thanks, Father!"

"I've made the exchange."

"Yes, that's your business," said his wife, and with her arms about him she paid no heed either to the sack or to the strangers.

"I exchanged the horse for a cow!"

"Thank God for the milk!" said his wife, "now we shall have dairy food, butter and cheese on our table. That was a fine exchange!"

"Yes, but then I exchanged the cow for a sheep!"

"But that was even better!" said his wife. "You're always thoughtful: we've got just the right grazing for a sheep. Now we shall have sheep's milk and sheep's cheese and woollen stockings, even woollen nightshirts! You don't get them from a cow, it just loses its hair. You're a thoughtful man if ever there was one!"

"But I exchanged the sheep for a goose!"

"You mean we'll really have a goose for Martinmass, my dear Father? You always think of my pleasure, that was a sweet thought of yours. The goose can be tethered and be fattened up for Martinmas."

"But I exchanged the goose for a hen!" said her husband.

"A hen! That was a good exchange," said his wife, "the hen lays eggs, it hatches them and we have chicks and soon we'll have a whole hen-yard. That's just what I've always wanted!"

"Yes, but I exchanged the hen for a sack of rotten apples!"

"Now you shall have a kiss!" said his wife. "Thank you, my own dear husband. I'm going to tell you something now. When you were away I was thinking about preparing a proper meal for you: omelet and chives. I had the eggs but I needed chives, so I went over to the schoolmaster's house. I know they've got chives, but his wife is a stingy old beast and when I asked to borrow some chives – 'Borrow?' said she. 'There's nothing growing in our garden, not even a rotten apple! I can't even lend you that!' And now I can lend her ten, or even a sackful! Oh Father, what fun!" And she kissed him full on the mouth.

"I like that!" said the Englishmen, "downhill all the way and happy all the same – it's worth the money!" And they paid over a shippound of gold coins to the farmer who had been kissed instead of cuffed.

Yes, it always pays for a wife to tell the world that Father knows best and always does what's right.

There, that was a story! I heard it when I was a little boy and now that you've heard it too, you know that what Father does is always right!

# The Swineherd

Once upon a time there was a poor prince. He had a kingdom that was very small, but it was big enough to marry on and that was what the prince wanted.

Now it was no doubt rather cheeky of him to dare to ask the emperor's daughter if she would have him. But dare he did, for his name was renowned far and wide and a hundred princesses would have said yes, but did this one?

We shall soon know.

On the grave of the prince's father grew a rose tree, such a beautiful tree, though it bloomed only once in five years and then produced only one flower, but that one rose was so fragrant that its scent banished all sorrows and cares. He also had a nightingale that could sing as if all the beautiful melodies in the world lived inside its little throat. He decided to present the rose and the nightingale to the princess, so both were placed in great silver caskets and sent to her.

The emperor had them brought before him in the great hall where the princess was playing at tea-parties with her ladies-in-waiting – they never did anything else – and when she saw the caskets containing the presents she clapped her hands with glee.

"Oh, I do hope it's a little pussycat," she said, but out came the beautiful rose.

"Isn't it prettily made!" said all the ladies-in-waiting.

"It is more than pretty," said the emperor, "it is nice."

But the princess felt it and almost burst into tears.

"Ugh, Papa," she said, "it's not artificial, it's *real!*"

"Ugh!" said all the courtiers, "it's real."

"First let us see what is in the other casket, before we get too annoyed," said the emperor, and out came the nightingale, which sang so beautifully that no one could say anything bad about it.

"*Superbe! Charmant!*" said the ladies-in-waiting, for they all spoke French, each one worse than the next.

"How the bird reminds me of her late majesty the empress's musical-box," said one old courtier. "Ah yes! The tone, the execution are just the same."

"Yes!" said the emperor, weeping like a baby.

"But I should not think it is real," said the princess.

"It is, it's a real bird," said the men who had brought it.

"Then let the bird fly," said the princess, and she absolutely refused to allow the prince to come.

But he was not to be discouraged. Smearing his face brown and black, he pulled a cap down over his head and knocked at the palace door.

"Good day, Emperor!" he said, "how about taking me into service at the palace?"

"Well, so many people come asking," said the emperor, "but let me see – I do need some-one to look after the pigs, we have such a lot of them."

So the prince was employed as the imperial swineherd. He was given a miserable little room down by the pig-sty and there he could stay, but he worked away all day long and by evening he had made a charming little cooking-pot with bells fixed all round it and as soon as the pot boiled the bells tinkled out the old song:

Oh, my dearest Augustine,
Everything's gone, gone, gone!

But the cleverest thing about it was that, if you held your fingers in the steam from the pot, you could smell at once what was being cooked in every hearth in the town – ah, that was something different from a rose!

The princess came walking by with all her ladies-in-waiting and when she heard the tune she stopped, looking pleased, for she too could play "Oh my dearest Augustine" on the piano. It was the only tune she could play and she played it with one finger.

"That's the one I can play," she said, "he must be a well-educated swineherd. Go in and ask him the price of that instrument!"

117

One of the ladies-in-waiting had to go in, but she slipped on a pair of clogs first.

"What do you want for that pot?" asked the lady-in-waiting.

"I want ten kisses from the princess," said the swineherd.

"Good heavens!" said the lady-in-waiting.

"I won't sell it for less," said the swineherd.

"Well, what did he say?" asked the princess.

"I really couldn't tell you," said the lady-in-waiting, "it's too awful."

"You'd better whisper, then." And whisper she did.

"He's very rude," said the princess, walking away – but she had not gone far before the bells began to tinkle again:

"Oh, my dearest Augustine,
Everything's gone, gone, gone!"

"Look," said the princess, "ask if he will take ten kisses from my ladies-in-waiting."

"No thanks," said the swineherd, "ten kisses from the princess or I keep the pot."

"Oh what a dreadful bore it is," said the princess, "you'll have to stand all round me so that nobody sees."

The ladies-in-waiting gathered round and spread out their skirts, so the swineherd got his ten kisses and the princess her cooking-pot.

Well, wasn't that delightful! The pot was made to boil night and day and they soon knew what was cooking on every hearth in the town, from the chamberlain's to the cobbler's. The ladies-in-waiting danced and clapped their hands.

"We know who's going to have sago soup and pancakes, we know who's going to have porridge and rissoles, it's so interesting!"

"Most interesting," said the mistress of the imperial household.

"Yes, but keep it a secret, for I am the emperor's daughter!"

"By all that's holy!" they said.

The swineherd, or rather the prince, although they had no idea that he was anything

but a swineherd, never let a day pass without making something. This time he made a rattle which, when he swung it, played all the waltzes, jigs and polkas of all the composers in the world.

"But that is *superbe!*" said the princess, passing by. "I have never heard a lovelier composition. Look, you go in and ask him the price of that instrument – but no kisses, mind!"

"He wants a hundred kisses from the princess," said the lady-in-waiting who had gone in to ask.

"I think he's mad," said the princess, walking away, but after only a few steps she stopped. "One must encourage the arts," she said, "I am the emperor's daughter, tell him he shall have ten kisses, like yesterday, but the rest he can have from my ladies-in-waiting."

"Yes, but we don't want to at all!" said the ladies-in-waiting.

"Rubbish," said the princess. "If I can kiss him you can too. Just remember that I give you your food and wages!" So the lady-in-waiting had to go back to the swineherd.

"A hundred kisses from the princess," he said, "or to each his own."

"Stand in front of me!" said the princess, and all the ladies-in-waiting stood round her while he kissed her.

"What's all that commotion down by the pig-sty?" said the emperor, who had come out on the balcony. He rubbed his eyes and put on his glasses. "Why, it's the ladies-in-waiting at play, I must go down and join them!" And he pulled his slippers up at the back, for they were just shoes that he had trodden down.

My, how he hurried!

As soon as he reached the farmyard he walked softly and the ladies-in-waiting were so busy counting the kisses to make sure it was an honest bargain and the swineherd received neither too many nor too few, that they simply did not notice the emperor. He stood on tiptoe.

"What's all this!" he said, when he saw who was kissing whom, and he smacked them on the head with his slipper just as the swineherd was receiving the eighty-sixth kiss. "Get out!" said the emperor furiously, and both the princess and the swineherd were expelled from his empire.

She stood there crying, the swineherd muttered angrily and the rain poured down.

"Ah, how wretched I am," said the princess, "if only I had accepted the handsome prince! Ah, I'm so unhappy."

Then the swineherd wiped the black and brown stain off his face behind a tree, took off the poor clothes and appeared in his prince's robes, looking so glorious that the princess curtseyed to him.

"I have come to despise you," he told her. "You did not want an honest prince. You had no interest in the rose or the nightingale but you could kiss a swineherd for a toy. So now, goodbye!"

And he returned to his kingdom, locked the door and shot the bolt so that now she could indeed stand outside singing:

> "Oh, my dearest Augustine,
> Everything's gone, gone, gone!"

For, as far as she was concerned, everything really had gone!

# The Fir Tree

Out in the forest stood a pretty little fir tree. It was in a pleasant position, open to the sun and air, and round it grew many of its big companions, both fir and pine, but the little fir tree was so anxious to grow that it gave no thought to the warm sun and fresh air, it paid no heed to the children's chatter when they were out gathering strawberries or raspberries. Sometimes they would come over with a full crock, or strawberries bedded on straw, sit down by the little tree and say: "Oh, what a sweet little tree!" But the little tree never listened. By the next year it was taller by a new branch and the year after that by yet another, because you can always tell a fir tree's age by the number of branch joints it has.

"Oh, if only I were a big tree like the others!" sighed the little tree, "then I could spread my branches far about me and look out over the wide world from my tip! The birds would build nests among my branches and when the wind blew I would be able to bow with dignity like those others."

It took no pleasure in the sunshine or the birds or the pink clouds which sailed above it night and morning.

When winter came, and the snow lay sparkling white about it, a rabbit would often jump right over the little tree – it was most annoying. But two winters passed and by the third the tree was so tall that the rabbits had to run round it. To grow up, grow tall, grow old – they were the only things that mattered to the tree.

In the autumn the woodcutter always came to cut down some of the biggest trees; it happened every year and the young fir tree, which was now very well grown, shuddered as the mighty trees fell to the earth with a groan and a crash. The branches were chopped off until the trees looked quite naked, long and slender. They were almost unrecognizable by the time they were laid on the carts and the horses pulled them out of the forest.

Where were they going, what awaited them?

In the spring when the stork and swallows came the tree asked them: "Do you know where they are taken? Have you ever seen them?"

The swallows knew nothing, but the stork looked thoughtful, nodded his head and said: "Well, I think I do, for I saw many new ships when I flew back from Egypt. The ships bore mighty masts and I daresay they were your trees, they smelled like fir trees. They held their heads high, I can assure you."

"Oh, if only I were big enough to fly across the sea! What is it like, this sea?"

"It would take much too long to explain," said the stork, walking away.

"Enjoy your youth!" said the sunbeams, "enjoy your new growth, the young life inside you!"

The wind kissed the tree and the dew wept tears over it, but the fir tree did not understand.

Now it was Christmastime, when quite young trees were felled, trees often no bigger or older than our fir tree, which could not live in peace and quiet but was always wanting to be on the move. These young trees, and they were the prettiest of all, always kept their branches when they were laid on the carts and pulled out of the forest by horses.

"Where are they going?" asked the fir tree. "They're no bigger than I am, in fact one of them was much smaller. Why do they keep all their branches? Where do they take them?"

"We know that, we know that," twittered the sparrows. "Down in the town we look in at the windows, we know where they're taken. Oh, theirs is the greatest glory and splendour you can imagine. We have peeped in at the windows and seen how they are planted in the middle of the warm room and decorated with the most beautiful things, golden apples and ginger biscuits, toys and hundreds of candles."

"And then –?" asked the fir tree, trembling in every branch. "And then? What happens then?"

"We've seen no more than that. It was wonderful!"

"Perhaps I have come into the world to take that glittering path?" the fir tree rejoiced. "That would be even better than sailing across the sea. I ache with longing. If only it were Christmastime, now I am as tall and my branches spread as widely as the ones that were taken last year. Oh, if only I were on that cart, if only I was in that warm room, in all that glory and splendour! And then –? Yes, then comes something even better, even more beautiful, otherwise why should they decorate me? There must be something even bigger afterwards, even more wonderful – but what? Oh, I ache, I yearn, I don't even know myself what is the matter with me."

"Be happy with me!" said the air and the sunlight, "Enjoy your fresh youth out in the open air!"

But the little tree was not happy. It went on growing and growing, winter and summer it kept its green, a proud, dark green. The people who saw it said: "That is a beautiful tree!" and at Christmastime it was the first to be cut down. The axe cut deep into its pith, the tree fell to earth with a sigh, helpless and in pain, quite unable to think of happiness. It grieved at leaving its home, the place where it had grown up, for it knew that never again would it see its dear old companions or the little bushes and flowers about it; indeed, it might never see the birds again. The parting was far from pleasant.

The tree did not begin to recover until it was in the yard being unpacked with the other trees and heard a man say: "That one is splendid,

that's the one we want."

Two servants in livery came and carried the tree into a big, beautiful hall. There were portraits hanging on the wall and beside the big tiled stove stood great Chinese vases with lions on their lids. There were rocking-chairs, silk sofas, big tables covered with picture-books and toys worth a hundred times a hundred crowns – or so the children said. And the fir tree was placed in a big bucket filled with sand, but no one could see it was a bucket because it was covered with green cloth and stood on a big, gaily-coloured rug. Oh, how the tree trembled. What was going to happen? The servants and the young ladies all helped to decorate it, hanging little nets made of coloured paper on the branches, each net filled with sweets; gilded apples and walnuts hung there as if growing from the tree and over a hundred red, blue and white candles were attached to the branches. Lifelike dolls – the tree had never seen such things before – perched on its green twigs and, at its very tip, they fixed a big, tinsel star; it was magnificent, absolutely magnificent.

"Tonight!" they all cried, "tonight will be brilliant!"

"Oh," thought the tree, "if only it were night, if only the candles were lit! And I wonder what will happen then? Will the other trees in the forest come and look at me? Will the sparrows fly to the windows? Shall I take root here and be decorated from head to foot all summer and winter long?"

It knew a lot, but it had a bad bark-ache from sheer longing and bark-ache is just as uncomfortable for a tree as a headache is for us.

The candles were lit at last, so bright, so splendid that the tree quivered in every branch, causing one of the candles to set the green needles alight, which scorched it badly.

"God save us!" shrieked the young ladies, putting the fire out hastily.

Now the tree did not even dare to tremble. Oh, this was awful. It was terrified of losing any of its splendour, it was quite confused by all the glory. Then the double-doors flew open and a

whole crowd of children rushed in, as if they were about to knock the tree down; the older people followed more soberly. For a moment the little ones were completely silent, but then they shouted until the hall echoed with their joy. They danced round the tree, and one present after another was plucked from it.

"What are they doing?" thought the tree, "what is going to happen?" The candles burned right down to the branches and when they had burned down they were put out. Then the children were allowed to plunder the tree. They flung themselves at it so that every branch groaned and but for the string by which the fixed golden star was attached to the ceiling the tree would have fallen over.

The children danced round with their splendid presents and everyone forgot the tree except the old nanny, who walked round peering among the branches, but that was only to see if the children had left a fig or an apple behind.

"A story! A story!" shouted the children, pulling a fat little man towards the tree. He sat right underneath it, saying "We'll be in the greenwood then, and it will be specially good for the tree to listen, but I'm only going to tell one story. Do you want the one about Chicky-licky or the one about Humpty Dumpty, who fell down the stairs, but still won the throne and the princess?"

"Chicky-licky!" shouted some and others shouted "Humpty Dumpty!" In all the shouting and shrieking only the fir tree stood quite silent, thinking: "Am I not to be part of it all, is there nothing for me to do?" But of course it had already been part of it all and it had already done what it was supposed to do.

So the man told the story of Humpty Dumpty who fell down the stairs and still won the throne and the princess, and the children clapped their hands and shouted "Another one, another one!" because they wanted Chicky-licky as well, but Humpty Dumpty was all they were going to get. The fir tree stood silent and thoughtful, for the birds in the forest had never

told a story like that. " 'Humpty Dumpty fell down the stairs and still won the princess.' Yes, yes, that's how the world goes," thought the fir tree, believing the story to be true because the man who told it was so respectable. "Yes, yes, who knows, perhaps I shall fall downstairs and win a princess too!" And it looked forward to being dressed with candles and toys, gold and fruit the next day.

"I shan't tremble tomorrow," it thought, "I'll really enjoy all my splendour. Tomorrow I shall hear the story about Humpty Dumpty again and perhaps the one about Chicky-licky too." The tree stood silent and thoughtful all night long.

In the morning the man-servant and the maid-servant came in.

"They're going to decorate me again," thought the tree, but they dragged it out of the big hall, up the stairs and into the loft where they put it in a dark corner without a chink of daylight. "What does this mean?" thought the tree. "What am I supposed to do here? What am I going to hear?" It thought and thought as it stood leaning against the wall and it had plenty of time to think as the days and nights passed. Nobody came and when at last someone did come it was only to push some big boxes into the corner. The tree was completely hidden now and one might have thought that it had been forgotten altogether.

"It's winter out there now," thought the tree. "The earth is hard and covered with snow and the people would not be able to plant me, so I suppose they are going to shelter me here until the spring. How considerate, how kind people are! If only it were not so dark and terribly lonely – not even a little rabbit for company. It really was delightful out in the woods when the snow was on the ground and the rabbits came leaping by, even when they jumped right over me, but in those days I did not like it. It certainly is lonely up here though."

"Peep, peep!" said a little mouse which had popped out at that moment, and then came another little one. They sniffed round the fir

tree, slipping from branch to branch. "It's awfully cold," they said, "otherwise this is a wonderful place to be in. Don't you think so, old fir tree?"

"I'm not old at all," said the fir tree, "there are lots much older than me."

"Where do you come from?" asked the mice, "and what do you know?" They were awfully curious. "Tell us about the most beautiful place on earth! Have you been there? Have you been in the larder where there is cheese on the shelves and hams hanging from the ceiling, where you can dance on tallow candles and go in thin and come out fat?"

"I don't know about that," said the tree, "but I know the forest where the sun shines and the birds sing." And it told them all about its youth, the like of which the little mice had never heard before and after listening they said: "What a lot you have seen, how lucky you have been!"

"I?" said the fir tree, thinking over its own story. "Yes, all in all those were very pleasant times." But then it told them about Christmas Eve when it had been decorated with biscuits and candles.

"Oh!" said the little mice, "how lucky you have been, old fir tree."

"I'm not old at all," said the tree, "this is the winter when I left the forest, I am in my prime, it's only that my growth has been stopped."

"You tell stories so beautifully," said the little mice and the next night they brought four more little mice to listen to the tree and the more it talked the more clearly it remembered everything. "Those really were pleasant times," it thought, "but they may come again, they may come; Humpty Dumpty fell down the stairs and won the princess after all; perhaps I can win a princess too." It was remembering a pretty little birch tree which had been growing in the wood, and which was a real princess to the fir tree.

"Who is Humpty Dumpty?" asked the little mice. So the tree told them the whole story. It could remember every single word and the little mice were ready to jump to the top of the tree in their delight. The next night many more mice came and on Sunday two rats came along as well, but they said the story was not amusing and that depressed the little mice and made them think less of it too.

"Is that the only story you know?" asked the rats.

"The only one," said the tree. "I heard it on my happiest evening, but at that time I never thought how happy I was."

"It's an extremely poor story, don't you know one about meat and tallow candles? Don't you know any larder stories?"

"No," said the tree.

"Well, that's that then!" said the rats, and went home.

In the end the little mice left too and the tree sighed: "It really was very nice having those lively little mice sitting round me listening to my story and now that too is over. But I shall remember to enjoy myself when I am taken out again."

But when did that happen? Well, it was one

morning, when people came and rummaged round in the loft, boxes were moved, the tree was pulled out and thrown rather hard across the floor, but a servant immediately dragged it to the stairs, where there was daylight.

"Now life is beginning again," thought the tree, feeling the fresh air and the first rays of the sun – and now it was out in the yard. Everything happened so quickly and the tree forgot to look at itself because there were so many other things to see. The yard was next to a garden full of flowers, roses hanging, soft and fragrant, over the little railings, limetrees in bloom and swallows flying about, chirping: "Tweet tweet tweet, my husband has come!" but they did not mean the fir tree.

"I'm going to live now," it rejoiced, spreading out its branches, which were all withered and yellow, but it was lying in a corner among weeds and nettles. The tinsel star was still fixed to its tip and glimmered in the bright sunlight.

Playing in the yard were two of the jolly children who had danced round the tree and been so pleased with it at Christmastime. The little one ran over and pulled off the golden star.

"Look what I've found on that ugly old Christmas tree!" he said, trampling on the branches which creaked beneath his boots.

The tree looked at all the fresh growth and flowery splendour in the garden and then it looked at itself and wished it had stayed in the dark corner of the loft; it remembered its fresh green youth in the forest, the merry Christmas Eve and the little mice who had been so pleased with its story of Humpty Dumpty.

"Gone, gone!" said the poor tree. "If only I had been happy when I could! Gone, gone!"

Then the servant came out and chopped the tree into little logs – a whole bundle of them. They blazed up beautifully under the big copper, with many a deep sigh, each sigh like a little shot. So the children who were playing outside ran in and sat in front of the fire, looking into it and shouting: "Bang, bang!" but with each crack that was really a sigh the tree remembered a summer's day in the woods, a winter's night when the stars shone down; it remembered Christmas Eve and Humpty Dumpty, the only fairy-story it had ever heard and known how to tell – and then the tree was burned up.

The boys played in the yard and on his chest the little one wore the golden star which the tree had borne on its happiest night; now it was over and the tree was gone and the story too: gone, gone, as all stories must be in time.

# The Steadfast Tin Soldier

Once upon a time there were five-and-twenty tin soldiers who were all brothers because they were made from the same old tin spoon. They were shouldering rifles and staring straight ahead in their handsome red and blue uniforms.

The very first words they heard in this world when the lid was taken off the box they lay in, were "Tin soldiers!" shouted by a little boy, clapping his hands. They were his birthday present and he set them out on the table. Each soldier was exactly like the next, only one was a little bit different: he had a single leg because he had been cast at the end when there was not enough tin left. But he stood as firmly on his one leg as the others on their two and he was the one who became remarkable.

On the table where they stood there were lots of other toys, but the most striking was an attractive cardboard castle. Through the narrow windows you could see right into the rooms and outside there were little trees growing round a mirror which was meant to represent a lake; wax swans were swimming on it, reflected in the glass. The whole thing was very attractive, but most attractive of all was a tiny lady standing in the open doorway of the castle. She too had been cut out of cardboard, but she was wearing a skirt of the purest muslin and a narrow blue ribbon lay over her shoulders like a stole. On it was fixed a shiny sequin as big

as her face. The little lady had both arms outstretched, for she was a dancer, and one leg was lifted so high that the tin soldier could not see it and believed she had only one leg like himself.

"She is the wife for me!" he thought, "but she is very noble, she lives in a castle and I have only a box and, since there are five-and-twenty of us, there is no room for her. Yet I must make her acquaintance." So, lying down full-length behind a snuff-box on the table, he gazed at the elegant little lady who was able to stand on one leg without losing her balance.

As the evening drew on, all the other tin soldiers were put in their box and the people of the house went to bed. The toys began to play their own games, from tea-parties to battles and balls; the tin soldiers rustled in their box because they wanted to join in but were unable to raise the lid. The nutcracker turned somersaults and the slate-pencil amused itself on the blackboard; they made such a row that the canary woke up and began to chatter, and in verse, too. The only two who did not move at all were the tin soldier and the little dancer; she remained upright on the tip of one toe with her arms outstretched and he was just as steadfast on his one leg, his eyes not leaving her for an instant.

Then the clock struck twelve and the lid

jumped off the snuff-box with a snap, but there was no snuff inside it – only a little black troll, for it was a trick-box.

"Tin soldier," said the troll, "will you keep your eyes to yourself!"

But the tin soldier pretended not to hear him.

"You just wait till tomorrow!" said the troll.

When morning came and the children got up, the tin soldier was stood in the window and either because of the troll or because of the draught, the window suddenly flew open and the soldier plunged head-first from the third floor. He dropped with dreadful speed, his leg in the air, and finished up with his bayonet stuck between two cobblestones.

The little boy and the maid came straight down to look for him but although they almost stepped on him they could not find him. If the tin soldier had called "Here I am!" they would have found him but he did not think it fitting to shout aloud when he was in uniform.

Then it began to rain, harder and harder, until there was a real downpour. When it was over two urchins came walking by.

"Look there," said one of them, "there's a tin soldier, let's send him for a sail!"

They made a boat from a sheet of newspaper, stood the tin soldier in it and off he sailed down the gutter, the two boys running alongside, clapping their hands. Heavens above! What waves tumbled down the gutter and how strong the current was! After all, there had just been a downpour. The paper boat bobbed up and down and once or twice it spun round so fast that the tin soldier was quite giddy, but he remained steadfast, never changing his expression but looking straight ahead and shouldering his rifle.

All of a sudden the boat rushed in under a long duckboard where it was as dark as the tin soldiers' box.

"Where on earth am I going now?" he thought, "oh yes, it's all the troll's fault, oh, if only the little lady were in the boat with me it could be twice as dark for all I'd care!"

At that moment a big water-rat which lived under the duckboard came forward. "Got your passport?" asked the rat, "hand over your passport!"

But the tin soldier remained silent, grasping his rifle still more firmly. The boat rushed on with the rat behind it, gnashing its teeth and shouting to the twigs and straw in the water: "Stop him! Stop him! He hasn't paid the toll, he hasn't shown his passport!"

But the current grew stronger and stronger and the tin soldier had already caught a glimpse of daylight ahead where the board ended, but he could also hear a roaring sound which might have terrified the bravest man. For where the duckboard ended the gutter ran out into a broad channel which was as perilous to him as it would be for us to sail down a huge waterfall.

He was already so close to it that there was no hope of stopping. The boat rushed on, the poor tin soldier held himself as rigid as he could – no one would be able to say that they had seen him close his eyes. The boat spun round three or four times and filled with water to the very brim. It was bound to sink now, the tin soldier was up to his neck in water and the boat was sinking deeper and deeper. The paper was falling to bits, the water rose over the soldier's head – and he remembered the charming little dancer whom he would never see again and in his ears rang the lines:

"On, on, you warrior brave!
Your goal shall be your grave!"

Then the paper collapsed and the tin soldier fell out, to be swallowed immediately by a huge fish.

Oh, how dark it was in there, even worse than under the duckboard, and it was a tight fit too, but the tin soldier was steadfast and lay full-length, shouldering his rifle.

The fish swam around, making the most extraordinary movements, until at last it lay still, as a flash of lightning seemed to strike it. The light shone in quite brightly and someone

shouted: "A tin soldier!" The fish had been caught, brought to market, sold and taken to a kitchen, where the maid had slit it open with a big knife. She picked the tin soldier up in two fingers and took him to the drawing-room where they all wanted to look at this remarkable fellow who had travelled in the belly of a fish; but the tin soldier was not proud at all. They stood him on the table and there – oh, what strange things happen in this world! The tin soldier was in the very same room where he had been before, there were the same children and the toys were still on the table, the beautiful castle with the charming little dancer still standing on one leg with the other raised high in the air – she too was steadfast. The soldier was so moved that he almost wept tin, but that would not be fitting. He looked at her and she looked at him, but they said nothing.

At that moment one of the little boys picked up the soldier and threw him straight into the stove without even giving a reason: the troll in the snuff-box was probably to blame.

The tin soldier glowed with a heat that was quite terrible, but whether it was the heat of the fire or of his love he did not know. His colours had already run, but none could say if it had happened on his journey or as the result of his grief. He gazed at the little lady, she gazed at him, and he felt himself melting, but still he stood steadfastly upright, shouldering his rifle. Suddenly a door opened, the draught caught the dancer and she flew like a sylph straight into the stove beside the soldier, where she blazed up and was gone. The tin soldier melted into a little lump and when the maid was emptying out the ashes next day she found him in the form of a little tin heart, but all that was left of the dancer was the sequin and that was burned black as coal.

# The Shepherdess and the Chimney-sweep

Have you ever seen a really old wooden cabinet, black with age and covered with carved scrolls and foliage? One just like that was standing in a certain living-room. It was a legacy from some grandparents and was carved from top to bottom with roses and tulips; among all the wonderful scroll-work little deer with antlers on their heads peeped out; but in the very middle was carved the figure of a man who was an extraordinary sight to see. He wore a grin – you could not have called it a smile – he had goat's legs, little horns on his head and a long beard. The children in that room always called him Goatlegscommander-in-chief generalwarofficersergeant, because that was a difficult name to say and not many people have that title, but carving him was quite a job too. Yet there he was, always staring across at the table under the looking-glass where a delicate little porcelain shepherdess stood. Her shoes were gilded, her skirt prettily gathered up with a red rose and she had a gold hat and carried a shepherd's crook. She was beautiful! Close beside her stood a little chimney-sweep, clothed in black, but made of porcelain too. He was just as neat and clean as anyone else and he was only playing at being a chimney-sweep. The porcelain-maker might as well have made

him a prince, for he looked just like one.

There he stood, holding his ladder, charming as you please, with a face as pink and white as a girl's, which was surely a mistake, for it should really have been just a little bit black. He stood very close to the shepherdess. Both of them had been placed where they now stood and since that was so they had become engaged to be married – they suited each other, they were two young people made of the same porcelain and both equally fragile.

Close by them there was another figure, three times as big, an old Chinaman who could nod his head. He too was made of porcelain and he said that he was the little shepherdess's grandfather, but he could not prove it. He claimed to have power over her and that was why he had nodded when the Goatlegscommander-in-chief generalwarofficersergeant had asked for the little shepherdess's hand.

"There's a husband for you," said the old Chinaman, "a husband who I really believe is made of mahogany, who can make you Mrs. Goatlegscommander-in-chiefgeneralwarofficer sergeant, for he has a whole cabinet full of silver quite apart from the things he has hidden away."

"I don't want to go into that dark cabinet,"

said the little shepherdess. "I have heard tell that he has eleven porcelain wives hidden away in there!"

"Then you can be the twelfth," said the Chinaman. "Tonight, as soon as the old cabinet creaks, you shall be married, as sure as I'm a Chinaman!" And he nodded his head and fell asleep.

But the little shepherdess wept and gazed at her best-beloved, the porcelain chimney-sweep.

"I believe I must beg you," she said, "to go with me out into the wide world, for we cannot stay here!"

"I want whatever you want," said the little chimney-sweep, "let us go at once. I am sure I can keep you, with my profession!"

"If only we could get off the table," said she. "I shall not be happy until we are out in the wide world!"

He comforted her and showed her where to place her little foot on the carved edges and gilded foliage on the table leg and by using his ladder as well they reached the floor, but when they looked across at the old cabinet there was such a commotion! All the carved deer were stretching their heads further out, lifting their antlers and turning their necks. The Goatlegs commander-in-chiefgeneralwarofficersergeant leaped in the air, shouting across to the old Chinaman: "They're running away! They're running away!"

Rather frightened now, they jumped quickly into a low drawer.

In it lay three or four incomplete packs of cards and a little puppet theatre which was set up as well as it could be in there. The puppets were performing a play and all the queens, whether of diamonds or hearts, clubs or spades, were sitting in the front row fanning themselves with their tulips and just behind them stood all the knaves, showing that they had heads top and bottom, as playing-cards do. The play was about two people who were not allowed to marry and it made the shepherdess cry, for it was just like her own story.

"I cannot bear this!" she said. "I must get

out of the drawer." But when they reached the floor and looked up at the table, the old Chinaman had woken up and was rocking his whole body to and fro, for his base was a single lump.

"The old Chinaman is coming!" cried the little shepherdess, falling on her porcelain knees in her distress.

"I have an idea!" said the chimney-sweep. "Let us crawl down into the big potpourri jar in the corner. We can lie on a bed of rose petals and lavender and throw salt in his eyes if he comes."

"That is no good," she said, "and besides, I know that the old Chinaman and the potpourri jar were once engaged and there is always a little kindness left after such a relationship; no, there is nothing for it, we must go out into the wide world!"

"Are you really brave enough to go out into the wide world with me?" asked the chimney-sweep. "Have you thought how big it is and that we shall never be able to return?"

"I have," she said.

The chimney-sweep looked straight at her for a moment. Then he said: "My way is by the chimney, are you really brave enough to crawl with me through the stove, across the body of it and up the flue? Then we shall be in the chimney and I know what to do there. We shall climb so high that they cannot reach us and up at the top there is a hole which leads out into the wide world."

He led her to the door of the stove.

"It looks black in there," she said, but she went with him through the body of the stove and up through the flue, where it was pitch-black night.

"We are in the chimney now," he said, "and look! The most beautiful star is shining above us!"

There really was one star in the sky which was shining straight down at them, as if to show them the way. So they crept and they crawled, it was a dreadful journey, higher and higher, but he lifted her and eased her way, held her and showed her the best places to put her little

porcelain feet and at last they reached the rim of the chimney, where they sat down, for they were tired now, as well they might be.

They had the sky with all its stars above them and all the rooftops of the town beneath; they could look out to far horizons. The poor little shepherdess had never thought it would be like this and she laid her little head on her chimney-sweep's shoulder and wept until the gold fell from her sash.

"It is all too much!" she said, "I cannot bear it. The world is much too big. If only I were back on the little table under the looking-glass! I shall never be happy until I am there again. Now I have followed you out into the wide world, so you can take me home again if you love me at all!"

The chimney-sweep reasoned with her, reminding her of the old Chinaman and the Goatlegscommander-in-chiefgeneralwarofficer sergeant, but she sobbed so dreadfully and kissed her little chimney-sweep so that he could do nothing but obey her, although he did not want to go.

Down the chimney they crawled with the greatest difficulty and through the flue and along the cylinder they crept, it was no fun at all, until they were standing in the dark stove. There they crouched behind the door, waiting to see what was going on inside the room. There was complete silence. They peeped out – oh, there in the middle of the floor lay the old Chinaman, who had fallen off the table when he tried to follow them and lay broken in three. His body was just a couple of lumps and his head had rolled into a corner. The Goatlegs commander-in-chiefgeneralwarofficersergeant was standing where he had always stood, thinking hard.

"This is awful!" said the little shepherdess. "My old grandfather has broken to bits and it's our fault. I shall never survive it," and she wrung her tiny little hands.

"They can still rivet him," said the chimney-sweep, "he can perfectly well be riveted. Please don't make such a fuss! If they glue his back up and put a good rivet in his neck he will be as good as new and able to say lots of nasty things to us!"

"Do you think so?" she said, and back they climbed to the table where they had been standing before.

"There, that's how far we went!" said the chimney-sweep. "We could have saved ourselves all that unpleasantness."

"If only poor old grandfather can be put together!" said the shepherdess. "Will it be very expensive?"

And riveted he was: the family had his back glued together, he was given a good rivet in the neck and was as good as new except that he could never nod again.

"You've become very haughty since you fell to bits!" said the Goatlegscommander-in-chiefgeneralwarofficersergeant, "but I don't think that's anything to be proud of! Shall I have her, or shall I not?"

The chimney-sweep and the little shepherdess gazed pathetically at the old Chinaman. They were very much afraid that he was going to nod, but he could not and he found it disagreeable to have to tell a stranger that he had a permanent rivet in his neck. So the porcelain people stayed together and they blessed grandfather's rivet and loved each other until they broke in pieces.